1862

"A CIVIL WAR LOVE STORY"

James Marquis

1862
"A CIVIL WAR LOVE STORY"

James Marquis

FORWARD

1862 is the forbidden love story that involves Confederate soldiers, slaves, and a couple of rednecks from Kentucky. Timed around the waning years of the Civil War on the Jefferson plantation, to which is the biggest and most well-known plantation in Louisiana.

The main characters find love and happiness at a time that is strictly forbidden. Death, disease and abandonment were obstacles that they must face as they push forward in their quest for adoration.

The author lets you live the trials and tribulations of each character as they face their journey in love. Each character discovers challenges in ways that bring out their deepest emotions, all while trying to find their perfect companion.

CONTENTS

1862

"A CIVIL WAR LOVE STORY"

Chapter I

THE BATTLE OF ANTIETAM

On September 17, 1862, in Washington County, Maryland, the Battle of Antietam was considered to be the bloodiest battle on American soil. Out of the 132,000 troops, 87,000 Union soldiers and 45,000 Confederates, an estimated 22,717 casualties were recorded in the engagement. General Robert E. Lee's Confederate army sustained 10,316 of those casualties and was ultimately pushed back into Virginia.

Coming out of unconsciousness, I realized it must be a dream, I could hear the muskets firing, cannonballs whisking overhead and hundreds of soldiers from both sides agonizing in pain on the battlefield. Instantly I felt a sharp pain in my right shoulder; looking down, I could see the blood leaking slowly through my uniform. Something must have pierced through my thick grey coat. A bullet? Shrapnel? At this point, it could have been anything. Raising my head, I could see the bodies of my fallen brethren lying on the ground for hundreds of yards around me. I knew this was not a dream, but reality.

Now fully conscious, I looked around to assess the predicament that I was in. I could hear footsteps in the distance, and as I investigated further, my heart sank deep in my throat! They were Union soldiers and marching in my direction! Each of them was equipped with bayonets latched onto their rifles, sticking corpses. Any Confederate soldier still living, they mercilessly executed on the spot. Despite being injured, my immediate attention was on my next action, fight or flight? For my very existence relied on this one decision.

Looking to the South, I could see a plantation tree, the ones that are tall, broad and covered with moss. It was only about twenty feet from me. I slowly crawled towards it, avoiding any attention and stopping every time the Union soldiers drew near. Once at the tree, there was an opening large enough for me to hide in. I propped a dead union soldier up to cover the opening of the tree after I crawled in. There, within the tree, I spent the evening still hearing voices and gunshots. That day turned into night, that night into the next day and finally on the following night when I decided to make my move before they begin collecting all of their fellow compatriot's bodies. With the soldier still covering me, I searched the body for any usable items. I lucked out and found half of a trampled first aid kit buried under the mangled top half of a fellow soldier, which contained iodine and wound coverings.

The second item I recovered must have been his pistol, for it too was covered in shrapnel and burnt a little, but it still looked like it had some function left in it. The gun was empty; yet, I was lucky enough to come across a spare container on a Yankee's belt that had four extra cartridges, which I immediately loaded into the pistol.

During this time, I was assessing my geographical location. We had been fighting the northern troops from the Potomac; they had marched forward towards Washington, DC, leaving the Potomac River and Virginia seemingly free for Confederate soldiers to regroup for the winter.

Now was my chance to cross the Potomac and meet up with my fellow soldiers and get the medical attention I desperately needed for my wound. As I proceeded to the Potomac, I followed the wagon road that was a designated passageway between Maryland and Virginia, hugging the tree lines. I stayed low and out of sight and always traveled only by night, always looking out for union guards.

When I reached the heavily guarded Potomac bridge, there was no way for me to cross it. So, I moved on and forged upstream until I came across a small hand-drawn ferry that could hold about four horses or one carriage at a time. The ferry was not operational at night and was secured on the Maryland side of the Potomac until daybreak. When I arrived under cover of a cloudy night, I was able to untie the ferry from its mooring and quietly forge my way across the Potomac.

I immediately moved into the thick brush and made my journey southward into the woods. The woods were pitch black, and the only thing to be heard was my own heavy panting and the earth occasionally cracking underneath my boots.

As I moved through the woods, I hear a loud snap and suddenly the sound of a bush moving nearby. I stopped in my tracks, slowly taking out my pistol and cocking back the hammer. Snap, another branch broke, but I heard now what sounds like the beating of hooves. Could it be Union Calvary? No, I would listen to more sets of horse hooves, and they wouldn't dare venture out this far into the sticks. Could it be a civilian? But wouldn't he have a lamp to illuminate his way through this rough? Before my next thought could even come to mind, a towering dark figure came bursting through the darkness. I aimed and was about to shoot when it stopped.

Good lord, it was just a horse! My heart was throbbing so hard the sound alone could give my position away! "Where did you come from friend," I said softly to the horse. It looked like a trader's stead with a saddlebag still attached to it. Forging through the bag, I discovered a map, a compass, half a flask of bourbon, and some jerky. I decided to camp there with the horse and ride out the next day.

When morning came, I took a look at the map, recognizing some of the land formations and continued to ride south. I had no clue if Union soldiers continued their push forward into Virginia, so I wanted to head as far south as I possibly could. The way they decimated us in Sharpsburg, I was nearly positive that our strongholds in Virginia must have fallen as well. I kept pushing south aimlessly, not recognizing anything on my limited map until I eventually got to the North Carolina line.

Once there, I rechecked my map, finally starting to recognize some of the land formations and headed in the direction of the "Land of Eden," North Carolina. Before traveling any further, I had to attend to my wound because the sharp pain in my right arm was almost too much to endure. I ripped open the bandages and poured iodine into the wound, but the bleeding did not stop.

I must have opened up the injury when taking off the crusty gauze, and if I could not stop or slow down the bleeding soon, I would be dead. I did the only thing I could think of and took out my powder pouch and poured the powder in my wound. Then I lit it with the flintlock of my pistol and nearly passed out from the pain. Luckily the fire sealed the wound and prevented it from bleeding any further. I do not know which was more painful -- the open wound or the process of sealing the wound, but I almost lost consciousness again and had to rest for the rest of the night before proceeding to Leaksville.

Chapter II

THE JACKSON PLANTATION:
Leaksville "The Land of Eden"

William Byrd II, a planter of both Virginia and North Carolina, owned 70,000 acres of land in which he wanted to bring many Swiss Protestants there and call it the "Land of Eden." He never realized his dream, and his son, William Byrd III, sold 26,000 acres in North Carolina to Simon and Francis Farley. In 1975 the town of Leaksville was established on the southwest edge of Sauratown.

*A*fter traveling a short while, I came upon an exceptionally large farm with slaves singing and working in the fields. In the far distance, I could see a pristine mansion and several outbuildings, which I would only assume to be slave quarters. As I was watching, I was surprised to see a regiment of Confederate soldiers approaching the main house and what appeared to be a General dismounted, greeted the owner, and had a lengthy conversation ending with a handshake. This act alone confirmed the reason why this plantation stood so pristine compared to all the other estates I came across in the South. An influential person must own it for the Confederate army to guard it so closely.

I thought to myself that I might get help here. Using extreme caution and the darkness to hide my approach, I came to one of the slave's cabins. I knocked quietly on the door, and a woman answered, saw my bloody uniform, and wanted to know if I needed any help. I told her yes. I went ahead and identified myself as a Sergeant in the Confederacy and that I had just been in a battle north of the Potomac and had a gunshot wound in my right shoulder that needed treatment right away. I asked if there was a doctor in this town. She said that I was in luck for they had a doctor on the plantation.

She walked me to the barn where a young black man greeted me. She informed him that I had been shot and needed treatment. He told me to follow him, which I did, to a small room in the back of the barn that was very clean and well-appointed with medical equipment and an operating table. He took my shirt off to assess the damage.

"That bullet has to come out, or you will get an infection and could lose your right arm. You did well in keeping the wound clean for all this time," he said as he continued to explore the wound.

"It seems I have a major decision to make, but before I do, may I inquire as to what your name may be?" I asked.

"Michael," he said.

"Well, Michael, I'm Jim, and I'm from Kentucky and joined the Confederacy along with two of my friends. They are missing, hopefully not killed. I just finished the deadliest battle I have ever been a part of near Sharpsburg and have traveled a great distance to get here. I am grateful for any help that you can give me."

"Michael, where were you schooled in the area of medicine?" He told me that he was a trained caregiver for the blacks that needed medical care.

"By the way Jim, Michael replied, you are probably one of the most well-spoken southerners that I have ever came across. Did you attend some schooling yourself?"

I told him that I was one of three cadets that went to the Kentucky Military Institute that made Sergeant as soon as I joined the war. The other two were my friends that I mentioned earlier, we all met in KMI. Michael smiled and replied, "hmm, now that makes a lot of sense, I was wondering why you seemed so poised."

"But we better get on with taking care of your arm, Jim. We don't want any infection setting in," he said as he laid me down on the table under an operating light and applied some type of smelly liquid under my nose, which made me very druggy, then proceeded to remove the bullet. Be assured it was not without pain, but shortly after, he bandaged up my right arm and put it into a sling.

"You are on the mend now. All you need is rest for two to three weeks." After the surgery, Michael washed all of the medical equipment and sanitized it with alcohol. He then meticulously put all the equipment back in its proper location in the cabinets of the operating room. Michael looked as if he was sixteen or seventeen years old, so young for a practicing caregiver. I finally asked him how old he was, and he replied twenty-seven, to my surprise. I then asked him where he learned to practice medicine? He said it was quite an interesting story for the owners of the plantation needed a full-time doctor, and he had always expressed interest in becoming one. They ended up sending him to study medicine for two and a half years with a doctor in Hartford, North Carolina.

Now he serves as the plantation physician for the slaves and the owners of the plantation as well. Sometimes he's dispatched to the owners of the other plantations in the area when the local doctor is not available. He is widely known for his medical training in and around Leaksville.

Michael also told me that he was born and raised on the plantation, and in fact, his mother still lives here.

"She is the chief cook for the big house," he proudly exclaimed.

He was half black and half white, so his coloring was a delicious milk chocolate color. The owner of the plantation treated all of the slaves and workers with respect and dignity. They received better food and lodging than any of the other plantations in the area.

My mind had so many unanswered questions; Michael's rearing was not typical of a slave. He was very handsome, light-skinned, tall, thin, and moved with the grace of a well-mannered person. I couldn't help but ask him how he was raised?

"Most of my life has been spent in the big house because that's where my mother works. Samuel Jackson, the owner of the plantation, treats me like a son even though he has two twin sons of his own by the name of Damian and Dan." Michael said the three of them were like brothers and that Damian and Dan were twenty-four, so only three years separated them.

As I surveyed the operating room, I asked where he lived. He directed me to his private quarters, and I was taken aback by its elegance. It held the finest in carpets, furnishings, lighting, and the most exquisite clothing that I have ever seen before filled his closets. His room even had its own private bath. After taking in all of this finery, I asked Michael how this all came about.

"They treat me as a member of the family," he said. And, in return for using his medical education to help the plantation, he received a good life. Samuel, the owner of the plantation, takes excellent care of him and also enjoys the fact that Damian and Dan share such a close friendship.

"When the opportunity arises, we hang out together, we go riding, swimming, and have barbecues along with some of the other young and handsome slaves on the plantation for our own entertainment," Michael continued.

"Michael, now that you want me to stay for a few weeks, where am I going to spend my nights?"

He replied, "You may stay in my private quarters, and I will sleep in my operating room." I wasn't used to his way of living, especially being in the trenches for these last few years. Me a simple country boy now staying in these luxuriously plush quarters… this was all new to me. I offered to stay in the operating room, for I did not want to deprive him of his living facilities.

"No way!" he replied softly but sternly. He would not accept my offer. I felt that special concern that he had for me even though this is the very first time we have met. Now my feelings were deepening, and I was looking forward to sleeping in his bed tonight and enjoying his scent on his bed linens for the first time.

That night Damian, Dan, Michael and I sat around the campfire drinking whiskey, telling stories and laughing. Every time I chuckled; my arm began to hurt. This was fine with me because laughter was what I truly needed, and that friendship was what I yearned for after being alone for some time.

As the night grew on and midnight was approaching, I could feel the whiskey and its effect on my body. I was lightheaded and a little wobbly. I said, "Michael, may you please help me to my room? I'm not going to be able to manage it on my own without falling."

Sure, enough, he grabbed me by my left arm and eased me to my feet. Putting his arm around my waist, we took one step at a time until we reached his bedroom. When inside, he laid me on the bed and helped me take my clothes off, shoes first, as I drunkenly looked at him. He took a beautiful pale blue dressing gown out of the closet; it was embroidered with a thick silver band along all the edges and soft to the touch. After he had me strip to my underwear, he began to put the gown gently on me.

While sliding his hands on my body, pushing down the gown, I slowly started to get an erection. I don't know whether Michael noticed it or not, but he finished putting the dressing gown on me and tucked me in for the night. That night I got the best night's rest that I have had since leaving home. The smell and warmth of the pillow and the blankets swallowed me in comfort. It was like I was sleeping on a cloud that smothered me with love and protection.

Something very unusual was happening to me. I have never been attracted to a black man or any man for that matter. Here in just one night, I was surrounded by Michael, Damian and Dan; all three men seemingly cut from the same cloth, and each truly fascinating. My mind was left to wonder. I had a burning desire to explore this feeling more, but how? In the morning, Michael brought breakfast to my room, and we shared some coffee. He asked how I was feeling and if I wanted to take a walk around the plantation today.

I immediately agreed and asked how many acres the estate had. Michael's response was approximately 600 acres of prime land; they had 100 slaves to manage its production. So, after breakfast, we took off to explore some of the estate's grandeur. When we got to a small lake surrounded by a field of reeds, not too very far from the main house, Michael put a blanket on the ground so we could rest and enjoy its quaint allure. At that time, he looked me in the eye and asked me if I'd ever had a relationship with another man. I was surprised, but the question needed an answer.

"No," I said. "I haven't had a relationship with a man, but I can tell you right now that I would not be opposed to it. You are the kindest person that I have ever known, and if I may say so, the most attractive as well. Last night when you were dressing me, I got an erection. Did you by chance notice?"

"Yes, I did. That is why I dared to ask you if you had ever been with a man."

As the morning passed into afternoon, we walked around the lake and proceeded back to the big house. Michael wanted to introduce me to his mother, so we made our way to the kitchen. Once inside the house, it was unbelievable! Gorgeous dark mahogany wood encompassed all the eye could see with home furnishings you would only think a royal would own. This was American luxury. We continued to take a quick tour of the house before we headed to the kitchen. Extravagant furnishings were everywhere, from the rugs, wall hangings, pictures and silver, to the most exquisite furniture pieces that you could buy. I've never seen anyone like this before. Inside the kitchen, his mother was standing over the stove with a glowing smile on her face.

"How nice to see you, Michael, who's your friend?" Michael proceeded to tell her that he had treated me for a gunshot wound on my right shoulder. His mom assured me that he was the best doctor in the area, and she was confident that I would fully recover.

Just at that moment, Damian and Dan came into the kitchen. They were so happy to see us there and wanted to know what we were going to do for the rest of the day. Not having any plans, we decided to join them for a fun-filled afternoon, which stretched into the evening. Damian and Dan were a strange couple. Not only were they twins, they seemingly were lovers as well. Michael told me that growing up with them was exciting because almost anything could happen on any given day. The three of them together had shared many sexual encounters that only a few could enjoy.

Michael had never been in a romantic relationship before. Damian and Dan always treated him like a brother and have been looking for a special person for him. He also explained how difficult it is for black men on a plantation to meet anyone with an education or a future. I kind of laughed and told Michael that I didn't have an education either.

"I'm just a plain old red-necked Kentucky boy. I worked on my father's farm tilling the land and attending to our livestock, nothing much more than that. I guess I had a girlfriend or two while I was growing up. I had thoughts of men before, but fear always held me back from exploring that world. I never really had an opportunity due to where I am from; this world is considered dangerously taboo."

Michael put his arm around me and gave me a big squeeze and told me that it was about time that I get introduced to this dangerously taboo world of theirs. As night approached, Michael took me to his room and into the bathroom where there was a tall standing shower with all-white porcelain tiling decorated by stylish bronzed faucets.

"Well, it's about time we get cleaned up, Jim; we've had a long hot day. I'll go first, and then you can join me." He climbed in the shower, turned on the water and before my eyes, I saw the most beautiful man that I'd ever seen. His 6'1" tall, lean body, showing all of his masculinity, which was plentiful, now stood before me. Perfectly chiseled from head to toe, every muscle on his seemingly thin frame swelled. After he finished,

I climbed into the water; boy, was it frigid! I told him I was afraid the water was going to make my penis shrivel up like a little worm.

Michael laughed, "I'm not out for size, just quality, and all I see in front of me is a quality specimen of a Confederate soldier. Your hairy body and legs outshine my smooth dark skin, but together we make a beautiful couple." During the shower, we hugged and fondled each other exploring our bodies in anticipation of our night in bed.

When the shower ended, Michael grabbed me and threw me on the bed. We were both naked as a jaybird, and to my surprise, we were both ready for action. Michael didn't waste any time, for he knew that I was sexually immature and took the lead. He started at my nose and worked his way to the tip of my toes, leaving me in complete bliss and sexual delight. I was breathless; he was such a magnificent lover! I could not compare.

He whispered in my ear, which sent tingles rippling throughout my body, "Don't worry, Jim, I'll take care of you until you can take care of me." As the night passed, I felt his body snuggled next to mine in a full embrace.

I woke up the next morning, realizing that I had never slept so well in my life. The first thing he said to me was that he would give me some of his clothes to get me out of that battered military garb that I had been wearing.

"Soldiers come around here all the time, and I don't want them to be confused as to what your status was and why you are not on duty. I fully intend for you to stay here with me for the duration of the war if you don't mind, of course," he said with a wink.

Michael and I were about the same size, so his clothes fit perfectly, and never have I been so well dressed. Damian and Dan liked my new cleaned-up appearance and commented that I finally look like a civilian and would fit in well at the plantation. Mr. Jackson said the four of us were a good-looking team, and he would enjoy all of us hanging around together to keep the spirits high at the plantation during this depressing time. In a way, I got the feeling that he knew what was going on between Michael and I and his two sons. Mr. Jackson told me that if I should get into any trouble at all with anything around town, to say that I am an esteemed guest at the Jackson estate and just the mere mentioning of his name alone should clear up any misunderstandings. I could tell that Mr. Jackson commanded great power, and it radiated through his words.

That day we took the carriage and made a trip to the closest plantation which belonged to Mr. Jackson's cousin Jerome. It was much smaller and only had a handful of slaves. Michael gave me a quick tour around the property and introduced me to some of his friends, some to which he had doctored back to health. He then introduced me to Jerome, who was surprisingly nice. In a soft raspy voice, he told me that he was glad to see Michael had a new friend.

On our way back to the plantation, we stopped by the lake and spread the blanket on the ground. Michael had brought along a picnic lunch that he stowed away in his brown leather satchel. We laid there basking in the sun, taking off our clothes, and getting ready to take a swim when two strangers approached on horseback. These men were foreign to the plantation; Michael had never seen them before. They were rugged and real nasty looking, they did not appear to be soldiers; if so, likely deserters. They immediately asked why we were lying there naked. We did not give their question a response, as we did not need to; they were on our land.

"You know that you're on the Jefferson Plantation, and this is private property," barked Michael.

"We don't care whose damn property this is. Why the hell are you two naked? Are you two some type of faggots or something, boy?" the older of the two snarled.

With that comment, Michael and I stood up and proceeded to get dressed. The two strangers got off their horses and started to walk towards us, each of them brandishing pistols with large bowie knives attached to their hips. They had a look of pure disgust in their eyes.

One of them took out his pistol and looked us both square in the eye and said, "How long has it been since one of ya's sucked a cock faggot?" We were both speechless. I felt I was better prepared to handle this situation than Michael because the army trained me not to take shit but to give shit.

"Fuck off; you're on private property, and our field hands will be here shortly," I exclaimed and went on to tell them that our location was discussed previously with the farmhands and that they should be back any moment now to update us on their progress. I suggested to them that they should mount their horses and ride on, and all would be forgotten.

"If not, you and I are going to have a long chat with a short conclusion with or without a gun. So, if you think you are a big man with a gun, get rid of it, and let's see how big of a man you really are, cowboy."

The man holstered his weapon and threw it to the ground. He then swiftly approached me, but little did he know I was a brawler. He was down with one blow; I countered his first punch, and he dropped like I knocked his soul right out of his body. The other one momentarily shaken came towards me, fumbling and bumbling, trying to reach for his pistol. I took him with two quick hits; he stumbled backward and fell. When both were down, I immediately grabbed their pistols and told them to mount up and ride away or die today. Their choice. I kept both pistols as they slunk off.

I turned to Michael and said, "There are certain things that I can take care of, just as there are certain things that only you can handle." Michael replied without hesitation, "It looks like together we're a surprisingly good team, me being the brains, you the brawn."

When we returned home from the eventful day we had, we both hopped into the shower to get cleaned up and wash away the memory of what we had endured by those two hooligans at our lake. While showering Michael made love to me: he told me that he could not wait until we were in bed together. That night was the first night that Michael made love to me. It was a night that I would forever remember for the precious gift he gave to me. We did not merely have sex; it was love, too. There's just such a difference between the two, but together, it's magical. I could feel Michael's energy through his fingertips and all of his gratitude for today's safe return via his kisses. Never in my life have I felt this type of love, and it was beyond the bounds of euphoria.

The next morning, we rose to start our day of work. It was our usual morning routine -- coffee, a light breakfast with toast, and we would always discuss Michael's daily rounds. He said that he would be gone for four to five hours today and that I should get to know some of the others who work on the plantation and that Damian and Dan would make the proper introductions. So, after Michael left, I went to the big house to check on the twins. They were just getting up because they too stay up extremely late at night. I casually asked them if we could spend the day together since Michael was going out on calls for most of the day.

Wholeheartedly they replied in tandem, "Sure! We were looking forward to spending more time with you, so let's have some fun!"

After they finished their morning routine, we headed to the stables to pick up our horses. There were no carriages available at the time, so we rode horseback through the fields and hills on the property. When I got to the barn, I instantly turned around and told Dan to excuse me, for I needed to head back to my room to get my pistol. He immediately asked why I needed to carry one, as they never needed a gun on their property.

He asked, "What on earth was it around here that I deemed such a threat, for I know it's not the cooking." From the kitchen, Michael's mother yelled out, "I heard you, Daniel Pierre Jackson!" We both laughed. I ended up telling Dan all about the encounter that we experienced yesterday by the lake, recounting that I had to fight off two men that were not from around these parts and did not appear to be Confederate soldiers. I confessed that's why I wanted to go back to my room and get my pistol, for I am never going out there barefisted again.

Damian and Dan took what I said seriously and looked at each other. They immediately headed back inside the big house. Soon they emerged with their pistols strapped to their waists with big smiles as well. All three of us made off on our horses, letting the wind determine the direction we rode. Soon we came across a small home and barn resting by a pond that looked uninhabited.

Damian softly said, "Well, I think this is where Luke McDonald and his parents live. I haven't seen them for quite some time now." We all decided to go on down to the house to see if anyone was at home. We knocked, but there was no answer. We looked at each other and Dan decided to go in. When inside, we could immediately tell that something had happened because someone had trashed the house.

We walked outside and proceeded to the barn where we found Luke, his mother, and his father hanging by the rafters. Why? Who would want to murder a whole family in such a way? The three of us dug the family's gravesites and proceeded to bury the bodies and mark their graves. They deserved a proper burial, not to be put on display like that. Whatever animal did this didn't even try to hide the hateful act it had committed! I was enraged. I then wondered about the two men that Michael and I had met the day before. I brought that up again to Damian and Dan and I said I think we got a problem here on the plantation.

"With over 600 acres, that's a lot of land to cover, but we have something that most people don't have, over 100 slaves that could assist in covering the area quickly," Damian explained. Returning to the plantation, he held a meeting with the foremen. He asked for their assistance to guide their teams throughout the plantation and bring back any information on the two men that I described. The next day, the search would begin at sunrise. Each search party had been authorized to carry one rifle, and on the off chance that something happened or if they needed assistance, they were instructed to fire two shots in the air, and we would all arrive there to assist.

It was mid-afternoon the following day when two gunshots ranged out in the direction of the eastern pasture. Michael and I, along with a foreman, immediately headed towards the shots. Upon our arrival, we found our foreman and his team huddled behind several rocks pointing in the direction of a campfire that was still smoldering. They said the shots probably scared them off, but they had probably come upon their camp while they were still there, so they must be close by. I, being the brawn, and Michael being the brains, sat down and formulated a plan to encircle the area with our foremen and their teams and catch those two men in a human dragnet.

As soon as we had everyone assembled, we all fanned out quickly, Dan and Damian rode horseback in opposite directions carrying a foreman along with them to drop them off at the most eastern and western points of our dragnet. They, in turn, rode up to the most northern part to hopefully cut them off or until we could fully set our encasement of the area.

The dragnet worked as planned; we encircled the two men, they laid down their pistols and followed our commands to put their arms up and hands behind their heads. We began questioning them first, asking where they are from and what they were doing here. They proceeded to tell us that both of them were deserters from the Union army unit that fought in the battle of Antietam. We couldn't believe what we heard, for I previously told Michael that I was wounded in the battle of Antietam, and now I have in my hands two of the Union soldiers that I fought.

After returning to the plantation with them in tow, we had the cook prepare a meal for the Union soldiers. While we were waiting on our meal, Michael and I sat down and started a casual conversation to gain more insight into who we initially thought were delinquent thugs. We had learned that their names were Tim and Jason; they have both grown up together and work in a small town in Pennsylvania, working in a factory the next city over. Tim said that hey been fighting for over two years, or should he say they been struggling to stay alive for more than two years! And they were just tired of it all.

They wanted to have their own lives and knew that wouldn't be possible in the North for they did not want to work for any man they wanted to be their own bosses so together they decided to flee the war and run away to the South for in the South everything is freer than the North. They continue to talk about their friendship with each other and never a mention of a girlfriend or wife. They appeared to be incredibly happy together and closer than they wanted anyone to perceive.

Jason was the first to admit that he was sorry for the way that they treated us at the lake. In fact, they were jealous of our encounter together and didn't want to show it. I asked him about the family in the barn and if they did it or knew anything about it. Justin said that they had come across the house and barn, but the family had already been hung; they had nothing to do with it. Neither one of them liked killing, which is one of the reasons why they left the war and headed south.

As evening crawled to night, Michael led Tim and Jason to a relatively small room close to the barn that worked as a jail cell.

Michael told them, "Until we could trust you a bit more, it will be in your best interest to stay here overnight. We'll let you out during the day for then there will be one hundred eyes watching you." Tim and

Jason walked inside the small cell; it had only one bed but was relatively clean. Jason said, well, Tim, I guess we better make a night of it and enjoy it while we can. Both of them hadn't slept on any type of bedding in months. So that night, they tucked themselves in, rolled over, put their arms around one another and kissed each other good night.

Tim and Jason both hadn't shaven since they joined the army. Their long wooly manes were gruff but yet well maintained. Their bodies were remarkably similar. Jason was just a little bit stockier than Tim, but their height was similar, and they both were twenty years of age. Morning came, and Jason was up before the sun like always, opening the door and walking outside to see what the morning would bring.

One of the foremen came up to him and said, "Pardon me, sir, it's time for breakfast, may you please come this way." Everyone soon met around the table and was served grits and bread, and they were so hungry. Shortly after breakfast, Michael and I joined them and continued our conversation with Tim and Jason from the day before.

We went back in time as far as they could remember being together, letting them tell us of their adventures as kids growing up on a farm in Pennsylvania. Tim and Jason shared that they never been involved in a relationship other than with each other, and they found that the army was not conducive to their lifestyle.

At this point, Michael and I were beginning to feel comfortable with them. Later, Michael, 'The Brain,' said that we should use caution in trusting them. He said one would never know if they made all this up to get on our good side and take advantage of us. I asked Michael to plan some outings for the four of us so that we could test the waters, but always keeping safety in the forefronts of our minds.

We decided that the first outing would be held at the lake where we very first met Tim and Jason. Michael arranged for some farmhands to go with us to the lake carrying rifles in plain view for both our safety and a show of power. Michael told Jason and Tim to gather the horses and that he would go to the kitchen to have the cook prepare us some food for our outing. When I approached the barn, the horses were all saddled up except for the saddlebag containing our blankets. So, I asked Jason and Tim to go ask one of the servants to fetch it in the big house so we could have it for our trip. It was not long before Michael showed up with two saddlebags full of food. We mounted our horses and headed out to the lake for this, our first adventure.

When we arrived at the lake, we dismounted and told Jason and Tim to ride over to the other beach and set up camp. The day was sunny and hot, so Michael and I took off all of our clothes and were lying on the blanket enjoying each other's company, knowing full well that the farmhands were protecting us.

Tim and Jason appeared to be more in a conversation type mood than one of relaxation. They knew that they had to leave and go further south and possibly even Texas for their safety. But they could not make the trip without any money, and they desperately needed a plan, hopefully using the owners of the plantation as their bargaining chip. They have yet to formulate the who's and how's of the plan. Still, they knew they needed to do something soon but didn't feel that Michael and Jim were of enough value to the plantation to fetch the amount of money they needed. So, they had to develop another scheme for Dan, Damian or their father.

As the evening set in, all four of them rode back to the plantation. Michael and I retired to their private quarters, and Tim and Jason walked around the row of houses of the farmhands to formulate their plan. Jason's first thought was of the twins. He told Tim that if there were any persons of value there on the plantation, it would have been the twins because old man Jackson really doted over them, and they're obviously very spoiled. All they needed to do now was to figure out a way to meet up with them in a secluded location on the plantation. Tim grunted, "We need for that plan to be put into immediate action!"

That evening at dinner, Jason asked us when all of us were going to have our next outing and when we did, if they could invite along the twins Damian and Dan to join in. Michael said we would consider it and get back to them when we have decided. Later on that night, Michael and I discussed whether we should have the twins join us and thought that it would be a good idea, not only would it be the more, the merrier but also safer for it would be the four of us against the two of them. Little did we know the outing was being designed for Jason and Tim to get closer to their targets, the twins.

The next day we talked to the twins and asked them if they would be interested in joining the four of us on a horseback ride around the plantation. Damian was the first to respond with "that sounds like a great idea," and Dan followed with his nod of approval. Michael told him that he'd put something together in a few days and then get back to them. In the meantime, Michael continued his rounds, and I assisted the foremen with the farm work. Jason and Tim mainly stayed to themselves while working on various labor projects for the plantation.

Three days later, the plans had been made for today's outing. Six horses needed to be saddled, and Michael would see to it that food is prepared correctly. In the meantime, I went to my room to put on my pistol. I told Jason and Tim where there's were, and they were generally shocked that they were authorized to carry their firearms on the property. I would explain my reasoning for this to Michael later. His plan was for us to ride to the farm, where we found the three bodies hung by the rafters a few days earlier. Michael wanted us to assess the reactions of Tim and Jason when we all toured the property.

When we arrived at the farm, we all dismounted and proceeded to walk into the farmhouse. Once inside, we looked around a bit, and it was in the same condition as it was previously when Michael and I found it several days ago. While I was standing there, I observed Jason and Tim's facial expressions and body language, which, in my opinion, seemed very tense and anxious. We walked outside the house toward the barn near the location where we found the three bodies hanging from the rafters. I said, "Well, let's find out what's in the barn." Jason and Tim had zero desire to go in the barn. I looked at them both and asked, "Why not? I'm sure there's nothing in there." Michael, Damian, Dan and I went into the barn and looked around, trying to see if we see anything unusual there. Tim and Jason refused to join us. I now was very concerned that Tim and Jason were potentially the killers, and I had to be on my guard for everyone's sake while still on this outing.

When we got to the river, the six of us laid out our bedrolls; Michael and I, at one end, Damian and Dan in the middle and Tim and Jason at the other end. The sun was at high noon, and the temperature was probably well into the 90s. We decided to shed our clothes down to our underwear and take a dip. It became noticeably clear to me that the ex-Union troops were becoming increasingly involved with Damian and Dan. I was taken aback because the twins were very devoted to one another. I then began to question Tim and Jason's motives behind these obvious sexual advances. As the sun began to set, we all got dressed, mounted our horses, and headed back towards the plantation. When we arrived, Michael and I told Jason to take care of the horses as we headed to our private quarters.

Once inside, we discussed what happened at the river. What could be going on between the four of them? We felt we needed to talk to the twins about this and make sure they understand the danger that they could possibly be in. Later that night, we both went to the big house to speak to them. Once inside, we met up in the game room where we had drinks and started a detailed conversation about the events that transpired that day at the river.

The twins said it was kind of exciting to be experimenting outside of our relationship; that hadn't happened before. It was obvious that Tim and Jason were more than willing participants, Dan laughed. They were sweet, Damian replied, they questioned if we had any concerns and the possible harm they wanted to avoid between us all. Michael and I reinforced the fact that we do not trust them nor know them yet, and extreme caution should be used when the two of them are around them. After about an hour, we returned to our private quarters and cleaned up and went to bed for the night. Each night we slept together was better than the night before. Michael never ceased to amaze me; he was incredibly tender and soft. His smooth ebony body was so orgasmic that I could not stop enjoying him in whatever position it may be.

Chapter III

TWO BETRAYALS

Into our town, the Hangman came
Smelling of gold and blood and flame –
And he paced our bricks with a diffident air.
— Maurice Ogden, The Hangman

*T*he next day about midmorning, I saw Damian, Dan, Tim and Jason ride off together in the direction opposite of the lake. I was immediately concerned and told Michael that we need to do something, for I didn't trust what was going on. Michael summoned the foreman and requested three men to ride off following them wherever they might go. Midafternoon the foreman came galloping back, the horse was near exhaustion, meaning that he had to have ridden a great distance at a great speed. He sprinted to Michael, nearly stumbling with trepidation, and told him that the twins were in serious trouble. He informed us that Tim and Jason had kidnapped the twins and tied them to a tree about four miles from here. They had also captured one of the farmhands who tried to creep down and cut them loose. The foreman said he didn't know what to do, so he left the other farmhand there as a lookout and dashed here directly to alert you all.

Michael and I immediately went to the big house where he informed Mr. Jackson about the situation. We reported to him everything we knew about the strangers, our concern that they may be the killers of the McDonald family and the twin's lack of concern. We told Mr. Jackson that on the previous day, the six of us had gone out for a picnic where the two appeared to be too friendly with the twins, thus further drawing our suspicion. When I got to the part in telling him who these strangers were and where they were planning to go, west to Texas or New Mexico, Mr. Jackson grew furious! "Union soldiers on my estate!" Mr. Jackson violently bellowed, throwing down his glass.

I quickly interjected, "We suspect that they need money for their trip and are using the twins as hostages to get the money from you. As a fail-safe, we loaded their pistols with fake bullets, so if worse comes to worst, we may have the drop on them, but that's our only trump card. First and foremost, we all are concerned about your sons' safety, so the three of us need to make a plan and do whatever it takes to get the twins safely home."

We began by summoning the foreman to the big house. We instructed him to take another horse and to ride out to where the other worker was and take along a white flag. Have the worker with you approach the kidnappers to find out their demands. From there, we can assess the situation and see our best route to action. He took note of our instructions and returned later that night with a response. They instructed the farmworker to return in forty-eight hours by himself with $10,000 in cash, and the twins would be released unharmed. And if they saw even one Grayback in tow, they would immediately execute them both and make their dash.

"Are they daft! That is an absolutely impossible request to make in two days' notice," Mr. Jackson exhaled. "I couldn't raise $10,000 in cash, even if you have given me all year! All my money is tied up in land and cattle, and the harvest is yet to be completed. Son, what do I do? I may have at max $3,000 on hand at any given time; even then, I would need at least a day to collect it all. We don't carry a lot of cash here, for we are as almost self-sufficient as we could be as most things are supplied through our plantation.

That evening, Damian and Dan sat there, knowing that their father could not come up with $10,000. They thought for a minute and then Damian said, "Well, these two guys are gay, so why don't we play their game, too." The next thing out of Damian's mouth was, "Hey, I need to take a piss,"

Jason hollered out, "Do it in your pants." Damian responded instantaneously, "Could you at the very least come over here and help me take down my pants so I could take a leak?"

Jason got up and dropped Damian's drawers to his knees and lo and behold, right in front of Jason's eyes was a half-erect penis surrounded by loads of blonde pubic hair. Dan saw Jason's amazement and hollered out to Tim, "I gotta take a leak as well." Tim angrily got up and said, "Now what in the Sam Hill is going on down here?" He soon found out. Dan said, "Well, aren't you going to drop my drawers?" Tim stood there for a minute, looked at Jason, and then dropped them.

Dan's pants hit his knees. There in front of him was the same blonde pubic hair, but Dan's penis wasn't erect. Damian spread his legs and asked Jason did he like what he has seen? Being held hostage has always been a shared fantasy of ours, so may we please reward you? Have you two ever thought about a four-way? You can untie just our hands and leave our feet tied so we can't run away for that's all we would need. Tim and Jason looked at each other and quickly said, "Fuck it," in unison. They untied just their hands and stood there, hobbled at the feet. "Why don't you lay the blankets down there, so we won't be in the dirt, Jason," Damian said lustfully.

The twins both laid back on the blanket, and Tim and Jason both stood at the end, looking at them laying there, vulnerable. Being the brave young man that he was, Damian told Jason, "Take off your clothes, and join us." To the twin's surprise, both Tim and Jason started to unbutton their own shirts, and when they removed them, the twins had never seen so much pale white skin in their entire lives. Jason was about 5'11" and Tim 5'10"; both were more medium built, with long brown hair and beards. Their chests were covered with beautiful brown hair all the way to the navel. Other than their size, they looked more like twins than friends.

Then off came the gun belts, which they laid on top of their shirts. Their pants were the next things to go. One thing that can be said about Pennsylvania farm boys is that they are genuinely perfect specimens. Damian quickly acted first, for he thought he'd better put on a good show for his captors. Damian and Dan took the lead, and each began stroking Tim and Jason to the point of climax. Before anyone could climax, Damian and Dan suddenly flipped them over on their backs and fucked the breath out of their bodies. When the exact moment was right, Dan withdrew and flipped over to where the guns were at and grabbed both of them. He removed the ropes from his feet, untied Damian's as well, and then gave him one of the revolvers so they could both keep Tim and Jason covered until they figured out what they were going to do with them.

Once again, they sat down and began to talk to them. They explained to them that Mr. Jackson, the owner of the plantation, had previously been governor of North Carolina for four years, and he was extremely influential. The commanding general of the garrison around the plantation is Mr. Jackson's cousin, so needless to say, nothing moves around here without Mr. Jackson's blessing or approval. There would be no way if you left today that you would get out of this County alive no matter what you tried to pull. So, let's cut the bull shit if you may, be honest with us.

Tim defeatedly replied, "Well, we told you about our time at the Pennsylvania farm where we grew up together, going into the army almost by force and the battles we experienced. We covered the desertion all the way up until we met Michael and Jim at the lake that day."

"Our immediate reaction that day was that of fear, for if anyone found out that a couple of union soldiers where here, deserters at that, we'd be lynched faster than the hangman could tie his shoe. Until that day at the lake, we have been able to evade any personal contact with anyone. Jim's very first accusation of us was that we hung those three individuals at the farmhouse, just before we got to the lake. We told him the truth that we didn't do it. Yes, we were at the farmhouse and did see the three hanging near the barn when we got there. But we were only there no more than thirty minutes and left immediately. Like I said before, there was nobody around when we got there and nobody around when we left."

"We did end up on your plantation locked up nightly in a cell, which we didn't mind because we could enjoy our freedom during the day, great food, your gracious hospitality and your company. But unfortunately for us, we had this problem that we had to solve, which was how we are going to get from the South to Texas or New Mexico on our own with little cash to our name. That plan needed money, and we thought that money was going to come from this hostage situation."

"We would never hurt either of you because we owe you such a great deal, especially the love and affection you bestowed upon us. Is there any way that we can work this out?"

Dan said, "Ok, maybe we can strike some sort of deal since no harm was done to us, but you two have a lot of repenting to do." Suddenly there was a rustling noise in the bushes. Dan cocked back his pistol and said to Tim and Jason, "Are you two expecting company?" They looked at each other with a puzzled look and responded no. Dan crunched down, aiming his pistol in the direction of the disturbance while his brother fixed his gun on Tim and Jason.

"Don't shoot young Masters! It's me, your worker Will," he said as he emerged from the thickets. "I been on the far side of that large hill, out of sight under strict orders to watch what's going on till foreman Russ returned with news. I see that now they's the ones need'n rescue, so I come down figuring that it's safe now. I'll ride back to the plantation and…"

Damian interjected, "Now hold on now, me and my brother were striking out a deal with these two, and how I see it, we were the ones wronged, so we get to decide their punishment if any. Listen here; you go and meet with foreman Russ and have him talk immediately with Father. Let him know that his sons have everything under control, and you take back the other worker with you and inform everybody that the four of us will be back at the plantation in about four hours. While you are also there, tell Michael and Jim that we would like to talk to them when we arrive."

Will grabbed the other worker and set off to the plantation as fast as he could. Dan told Damian that he felt that during the next four hours that they both could formulate some type of plan that could benefit everybody at the plantation. Dan leaned over to Damian and said, "You know these guys used to be farmers back in Pennsylvania."

I wonder what they know how to grow? Damian said, "Now Jason, back in Pennsylvania, what did you guys grow? He replied, "Soybeans and corn, those are the highest yielding cash crops that you can get per square acre.

Dan then asked Jason, "Do you plant per acre per field? How do you budget all your seeds and material?"

"It's growing season right now, and I can safely project all the profits within a three-year expanse when properly budgeted, with the costs of this year you should make a 10% profit this fall after all your expenses; set up and vendor dealings. The first year is always the most expensive," concluded Jason.

Dan scratched his head and asked him, "How did you figure all this?"

Jason gave a slight chuckle and replied, "Well, we grew up dirt poor with lots of competition. The only way we could stay ahead of the other farmers was to outsmart them, for we didn't have the money to really compete with the bigger farms. So, we created a formula, one that I could prove to the banks so they would give us a loan to stay afloat until the next crop came in. I'm sure you must do some science here with this vast empire that you run. I can't imagine the plantation being managed on a shoestring or you all would be wasting money. Tell me how much you produce here."

Dan replied, "Well… I'd say about… one hundred acres of tobacco, one hundred acres of soybeans and corn, one hundred acres of sweet potatoes, and three hundred acres of cattle."

Jason immediately went to work crunching numbers and asking about supply lines and enhancements. It appeared to the twins that Jason's formula could indeed work on all of their crops. Now they had to deal with their biggest obstacle, talking to their father about today's events.

When they returned, the twins met him in the game room where they both poured themselves two fingers of bourbon; Dan's straight while Damian had his on the rocks, one of the only ways to tell the twins apart. They explained to their father that Tim and Jason weren't as they seemed. A series of unfortunate events led them down the wrong path to desperately acquire money to finish their dangerous journey. They had no one but each other and no proper guidance.

Dan stepped in and said, "Father. Michael, Jim, Damian, and I all enjoy the luxury of your beautiful plantation. We only wish to spread a little bit of our good fortune to bring happiness to the people around us. This is precisely what Jason and Tim are trying to find. As we all know, everything in life has a price, and every misdeed has to go punished."

"With that said, Jason has great knowledge about agriculture, and I believe that if you talk to him, you will find out how he can benefit our plantation. He has crafted a formula of sorts to enhance growth and production and has projected a large increase in our profitability this season. We can secure financing for further operations on the plantation. His plan all boils down to two things: field development, which includes better use of fertilizers, and a more advanced watering system that uses less water and better soil rotation.

There is a lot more that they do, Father, but you see where I am going with this."

"The second part of the operation," Damian continued, "is something that you may like a lot for it certainly caught our attention, the use of others' cash and products to make money. We set on a tour, enlisting businesses who sell items that we need and that any farm would need. In exchange for deeply discounted items, we will market these items to our vast array of contacts swearing by their effectiveness and how they increased our productivity.

Of course, we would be backed by the Jackson name and the fact that we are the largest plantation in the lands. After we utilize Jason's formula, they will see that we have significantly increased our production and profit but won't know what caused this rapid spike! All we have to do is tell people that 'this or that' is a miracle solution to all their farming needs, and people will fight to listen. Brilliant, isn't it? Father, I want to arrange a time for you to meet Tim and Jason, and then you can make your own opinion of the two and their skills. I promise you will not be disappointed."

The very next afternoon, Mr. Jackson met with Tim and Jason. Michael and I were surprised that they met for such a considerable length of time. After the meeting, the twins met with their father and asked him his opinion on Tim and Jason? He said he was quite impressed with the two, only saddened that they had to meet under these circumstances. However, he is glad they are prepared to atone for their past and are happy to join our plantation's production. He told me that he would give control of the rare unicorn operation to the two for a season and then evaluate the production from there to see if they are worth keeping on. He told the servants to find them adequate quarters and make sure they have no access to weapons and have the staff keep a close eye on them for a while we work things out. He also said that he would have the Sheriff investigate the McDonald farm but shield them from any accusations.

The twins told us of their father's decision, and they felt comfortable with it and believed that the six of us needed to have a long chat so we could have a better relationship with each other. Damian said maybe we could just arrange dinners a few times a week; that way, we will have them together and can keep tabs on what's going on in each other's lives.

Michael said, "That's a good idea. Damian, could you make that happen?" Damian arranged for Friday, Saturday, and the occasional Wednesday night for all of us to have dinner together. Each time we met the evening drug on and on and a few drinks turned to plenty, because there was always plenty of corn whiskey in stock.

One Saturday night, after we had polished off a bottle of whiskey, Damian and Dan invited us all back to the big house. Michael and I had been invited there on several occasions before, but it's grandeur never ceased to amaze me; it could only be described as pretentious. Eight bedrooms and baths, furniture that you couldn't believe could be crafted by men along with rugs from every part of the world. After a quick cocktail or two, Michael and I retired to our bedroom. Dan and Damian asked Tim and Jason if they cared to join them for a nightcap to which they obliged. I can only guess what went on in Damian's bedroom, but it must've been joyful because the next morning, the four of them looked exhausted, but all had great, big happy smiles stretched across their faces.

I had been at the plantation for two months, and Michael and I had settled into his room. It was so beautifully appointed with furniture from the big house. Our time together seemed more like years than weeks. We were so compatible in every single way imaginable, and with every day, our love grew stronger. Mr. Jackson valued Michael's contribution and treasured his good looks. He knew that Damian and Dan had a special love for Michael that went far beyond friendship. Michael and I had spent a lot of time with them even before our new relationship with Tim and Jason. I think that Damian and Dan were kind of envious of my relationship with Michael but were gracious about it and welcomed me into their family with open arms.

Damian and Dan, the twins, had explored each other's bodies since their early youth. They had grown up attached to the hip, and no one ever made any bones about it. Their father seemingly accepted this unusual relationship, but he did everything possible to keep them on the plantation and happy. He did not want them to go to war, for he feared losing one or both of them. Damian and Dan both stood about 6-foot-tall with short-cropped blonde hair, their bodies in the summer months of the year shined a golden hue, and they proudly displayed them with their shirts off most of the time while at work.

Michael and I never caused any issues within the household because we had a strictly monogamous relationship, and we were so in love with one another that any display of sexual energy from anyone else did not affect us in the least. But that wasn't the case with Tim and Jason; they were still sowing their wild oats because they had been very isolated on the farm in Pennsylvania and never had the opportunity to meet any other gay men.

Tim and Jason had settled into one of the homes in the Foremen section of the compound. It was very poorly furnished and not at all clean. When they both got off work, they would scurry around collecting pieces of furniture from various cabins to enhance the decor of their home. At night they would scrub the floors and wash the windows, and they even added draperies to make the place come to life. Their life together was now starting to transform. They were no longer the shy farm boys from Pennsylvania; instead, they were accepted residents of the Jackson plantation who were responsible for crops, budgeting, and social networking among his newly found friends.

They both agreed to use caution whenever they got into any sexual situation with the sons of the owner. They would have nothing screw up the newly found position and opportunity in life, so they agreed with each other that they should keep their noses clean and the pants zipped unless they were together when the event took place.

Every day started the same way, with the six of us getting together for breakfast and discussing our daily routines. Michael would always go first discussing his rounds for the day, then the following field assignments were discussed:

- Damian handled the tobacco crop, marketing and met with the foremen to assign their tasks.
- Jason handled the budgeting efforts and agricultural improvements.
- Tim handled the soybeans, corn and digging the water trenches.
- Dan oversaw the sweet potato crop and kept up with the affairs of the Big House.
- And I handled the 500 head of cattle, serviced and maintained the armory, and was put in charge of security.

So, our day started off very well organized, and each of us had the appropriate number of workers assigned to us with several foremen to help maintain productivity. As time went along, Jason had prepared all of his forecasts for the fall crops and cattle sales. When Mr. Jackson reviewed all of the statistics, he was overwhelmed to discover that his projected profit for the plantation would be tripled from its normal amount. He told Jason that if these figures become true that he and Tim would have a permanent position at the plantation from now on.

As summer turned to fall and the crops and cattle went to market, Jason's projection came in and was not in the least short. The plantation's overall profit for the season was four times greater than usual. Mr. Jackson called the six of them to the big house for a meeting. When we arrived, Mr. Jackson was in the game room, sipping whiskey by the fireplace, sitting in his favorite brown leather chair. He welcomed us most graciously, complimenting us all on our stellar work and, most of all, Jason on his calculations that led to the abnormal earnings of the plantation. It was at this time that he offered Tim and Jason a full-time paid position on the plantation plus improved housing along with any additional requests that they might have.

Tim and Jason were surprised and delighted that they were going to have a paid position on the plantation. By having this, they would be able to save enough money and proceed on their dreamed exodus to Texas or New Mexico. They negotiated the salary on the spot, then inquired about their living situation. Mr. Jackson informed them that he maintained a guesthouse that was not being used. He said it was nicely appointed and comfortable, that they should check it out tomorrow and let him know if that would be adequate.

Michael and I got up and shook Mr. Jackson's hand and told him that we felt like he made a promising decision and that we were thrilled that the plantation made a fantastic profit this year. Tim and Jason were ecstatic that they were being treated as if they were two extra houseguests here on the plantation. They thought to themselves what excitement this new position was going to bring to their lives. But in their minds, they couldn't forget that only months ago they had kidnapped the twins and were going to use them for ransom.

The guesthouse was quite nice, yet it had only one bedroom and no bathroom. There was, however, an outhouse just a short walk from the house. It hadn't been lived in for some time, so they spent their evenings once again cleaning and decorating, making their new quarters a wonder of comfortable. They were proud to have paying jobs, excellent living conditions, and a place where they could spend time together without interruption. With this luxury, Tim and Jason now had the time to explore each other's sexuality to its fullest. Jason usually dominated Tim in the bedroom as Jason was that bigger of the two and hung like a horse. Tim always willingly submitted to Jason's advances in the bedroom or living room or wherever they might be at the time with enthusiasm and kindness. Jason's creativity paired well with Tim's compliance, leading the two to create several lewd games, and for Tim, the more demeaning, the better.

A few months passed by, and all was going well on the plantation. Each individual was performing their assigned duties at their highest level and enjoying themselves together during and after work. Their weekly dinner gatherings were now being expanded from three days a week to every day. The six of them found that spending time together was very relaxing and comical in a way being that all of their different personalities were still eerily similar in a way and were able to joke with each other without being offensive.

A few more weeks passed, and Jason appeared to have more than a joking interest in Damian. Sometimes they would walk off together through the compound and simply vanish for one or two hours before mysteriously returning home. This became a nightly occurrence and also apparent to the four of us that remained. Tim never spoke of it to anyone, but Michael and I figured that he wasn't too thrilled about this budding relation. When we were alone, Michael and I discussed their little adventures and wondered if the two of them were starting to develop a closer relationship than they wanted to let on.

One day I asked Tim if everything was going okay with him and his relationship with Jason? He said that it seemed that Jason had become more interested in Damian and that the sex between Jason and him had thus been eliminated almost entirely. He knew that living here and getting paid to work was by far the most lucrative and comforting position that they ever held and what they have here is a once in a lifetime opportunity. Still, he just didn't know how to handle their relationship anymore. At first, I just listened, as a friend should. Not offering any advice but letting him know that Michael and I are here any time he needs, no pressure. I told him that it's particularly important that all six of us make the plantation work and keep it profitable.

That night I spoke to Michael about the conversation I had with Tim and that he was lost as to how to handle Jason's affair with Damian. He said he didn't want to lose him, but if he did, he would prefer losing him to Damian rather than some cowboy along the trail to where he would never see him again if that makes sense. Michael was perplexed as he had been around Damian and Dan his entire life and never known them to be involved with anybody else besides themselves. Maybe Damian's infatuation with Jason was just that, an infatuation. Or could they be in love?

The next day, I spoke to Dan and asked about his relationship with his brother. "What is going on between Damian and Jason?" Dan explained that he and his brother were all they ever had together for all these years and that Damian had found Jason to be not only smart but ruggedly handsome and sexually appealing. Dan said that Damian had been doing things with Jason that he had never done before, and he had been enjoying it and that our relationship was limited by lack of rugged sexuality and versatility.

"There is no way that I'm about to compete with Jason. All I want is for the six of us to be together here at the plantation and live happily ever after even if that means that Damian and I moved to separate bedrooms and let nature take its course," Dan said softly.

Within a few days, Damian talked to his father about the relationship he was involved in with Jason. Mr. Jackson was not surprised and only suggested that Damian take his time to make sure that this is what he undoubtingly wanted. He acknowledged that Jason was very much an essential part of the success of the plantation and would welcome his relationship.

Dan also was warming to Damian and Jason's relationship. He was growing fonder of Tim and in a way that he had not felt about his brother. Tim was more rugged and really a farm boy who liked getting his hands dirty. He wasn't clean-cut, and his outward appearance wasn't one that you would want to take to any social gatherings or other plantations without causing a stir.

Dan and Tim would sit evenings together talking about life and what Tim wanted to envision for his future, a future without Jason. Tim was rather perplexed at times, as a result of never being without Jason. One night after dinner, when they were alone, Tim came right out and asked Dan if he thought they could have a future together? Dan was surprised, and it took him a while to formulate an answer. After much consideration, Dan responded, "I think if we both give a little, something will happen." Tim quickly countered, "What do you mean by giving a little?" Dan replied, "I'm rather polished and sophisticated, and you're a cowboy through and through. If you accept me, then I'll accept you. When we engage with other people outside the plantation, let me take the lead in the conversation, and if you support me, and I think everything will work out okay."

Tim sighed, "So you want me to be your shadow, not your equal."

"No, that's not what I'm trying to say; we need to work as a team, each one using the best of what God has given us, and I think the best of you is hidden under all those clothes that cover up your manhood. You're far more of a man than I ever been in my relationship with Damian. He was always the aggressor, and I always followed him, and I'm just hoping that you would do the same to me. Put it this way, I want you to be my rock, and let my heart surround you."

Later that night, Dan made his way into Tim's room and spent the night. Or shall I say he spent a glorious night enjoying his hairy body and deep passionate sex? Never before had Dan's body had the pleasure to explore as much as it did that night with Tim. He was a rough and grizzled cowboy in bed, and that's what Dan needed. There was no doubt in Dan's mind after that spectacular evening of fire that the two of them would further add to the success of the plantation, and that was the bottom line.

It was late fall of 1862, and the plantation was humming with prosperity. All six of us, Damian, Jason, Dan, Tim, Michael and I, were focused on the aspects of quality and productivity. As part of the deal with Mr. Jackson, Jason would brief us about his research, teaching us little by little the methods that he uses while Tim demonstrated and explained how to use the new tools and systems. Michael's rounds continued to increase, requiring him to be away from the plantation a bit longer each day. I, on the other hand, had expanded the cattle operation by 100 head of cattle and cleared an additional fifty acres of land for grazing purposes. Tim and Dan were working jointly together on field operations so that Jason could spend more time teaching Damian accounting and budgeting. We were one happy family, and Mr. Jackson was more than pleased with the outcome.

Dan moved out of the big house into the quarters that Tim inhabited alone since Jason decided to room with Damian. He was extremely comfortable living with Tim and enjoyed the cowboy environment immensely. Michael and I were so happy being together that I felt that there was not enough time in the world with him that could satisfy me as days turned into weeks and weeks melded into months. Our love only intensified—all without a single curse word to be shared between us two or even a simple misunderstanding. Michael was the most incredible human being that I had ever met, beyond only handsome and sexy; he was so unimaginably intelligent. It was beyond words. Our life together was like a storybook, and I could only wish that this story would end with him and me.

Damian and Jason were incredibly happy in the big house. Jason quickly became accustomed to the fineries of life, and Mr. Jackson developed a great comfort in having Jason around. Although Jason was basically a wiz of a farmhand or a cowboy, whatever you want to call him, he was extremely neat, well-organized and intelligent. At this very moment, you would never be able to guess that this well-polished man came from a dirt-poor farm in Pennsylvania. Now he's dealing daily with bankers and other plantation owners with ease.

Now you may be asking, isn't this supposed to be a love story. My answer is yes, a civil war love story. May I first ask you what is "love"? I will describe my interpretation: when a kiss makes your toes tingle, when a passionate hug is your climax and when you look into their eyes, and you become one. As a poet once said, "For even as love crowns you, so shall he crucify you. Even as he is for your growth, so is he for your pruning." For love is like a rose; it needs both the sun and the rain, without this other side of love -- the fear, the anger, the pain. How is it that we would truly understand our hearts without feeling both sides? You may still laugh, but not with all your laughter, cry but not with all your tears, and love but not with all your heart. Would it even be considered love if it is not complete? The question in the story is who is genuinely in love?

Recently, Tim and Jason had been meeting privately after dinner on weekends. The longer these discussions went on, the more they focused on leaving the plantation and heading to Texas or New Mexico as previously planned. Tim would rationalize that it would only be a matter of time that someone found out that they used to be Union soldiers. This would not only put their lives in peril but also would jeopardize the operations for the entire Jackson plantation. They would be found guilty of harboring and embedding the enemy, thus eliminating all their monetary gains and could ruin them.

Tim felt that they could not allow themselves to be this selfish and needed to formulate a plan to subsidize their trip financially. Jason was a little more resistant to the notion, for he rather enjoyed the spoils of his new life, and moving west did not guarantee that he would even be a quarter as successful as he is right here and now. However, he had to admit that he never wanted to bring any harm to this plantation and that they need to work out a viable solution.

One morning Damian was thinking about how much their sex life had fallen off or declined lately with Jason. He was thinking about asking Jason if there was something that he had done to offend him in any way but decided to postpone that conversation. Later that day, Damian decided to take a break with his brother, and during their discussion, their sex life came back up. They found out that both of them were having issues with their lovers, and both discussed their mutual concern and how to resolve the issue. Neither one of them came up with a better approach other than to just ask, for there must be a simple answer to their question.

That night twins both asked their partners directly and received their response. The following morning Dan and Damian got together to talk about what transpired the night before. Both of them had the same answer: a little of this a bit of that; I'm tired, etc. etc. This answer did not suffice in the least. They both knew there had to be something going on. So, they agreed to keep their eyes open, as well as the plantation's many ears to the ground.

You know everything in life revolves in a circle. What came must go this was true even with Tim and Jason, for they still endeavored to head out west no matter how well the twins treated them. Damian and Dan both agreed they had a real problem. The first concern was with the bank accounts for Jason handled all of the receipts and transactions in billings etc. via the bank. When Damian decided to contact the bank to check if anything suspicious activity, he discovered that all of the accounts were practically zero. He asked the bank manager when all the money was withdrawn? He researched for the records and showed Damian that the money had been withdrawn only yesterday.

Additionally, it was withdrawn in all cash, not by check. The teller knew Jason personally but described the gentleman that he was with as a tall bearded cowboy with a complexion kissed by the sun.

On the way to the Sheriff's office, the twins wailed to each other that they been literally fucked out of the money their plantation made this season. Dan said, "We should split up, and after I file this report, I will head immediately to the plantation and help secure those damn Yankee thieves. You ride ahead to warn the others." With the necessary paperwork filed, Dan rode posthaste to the plantation. When he arrived, he was told that Tim and Jason had left four hours ago. Dan rushed to the barn to see if Michael and I were still there. Michael had left before Damian arrived to make his daily rounds, but I was still there, and Damian had already explained to me what the issue was. "We need to round up some farmhands and pursued them immediately," I shouted. I rounded up some twenty-four field hands had them armed and supplied, then we pushed southwest at full speed.

To our advantage, we were traveling on our 600 acres, and we knew it like the back of our hand, Tim and Jason were never the adventurous types, so they never went too far from the Big House. Traveling at night was not a challenge, and in doing so, we made significant headway in our chase. One of the field hands caught sight of the two as they approached Belew's Lake. We hurried down the mountain, taking a short cut that would cut the two of them off. When we finally caught up to the two, they both decided to flee at full speed. Not knowing the layout of the land and not being particularly skilled at riding, we quickly caught up them, and I pulled out my pistol and fired two shots missing both of them.

"The next shots will not miss I promise you that boys!" I yelled with great disgust. Jason, now terrified, stopped his horse, and Tim followed suit. I rode up to them gun locked on the both of them and said, "Let's make this quick and easy, we caught you bastards." We recovered all of the plantation's funds and tied up Tim and Jason, riding them back to town on the backs of our horses. Lucky for them, they were afforded the luxury of a trial by jury in the town courthouse. For me, I wanted to shoot them where they stood. I never gave anyone the luxury of fooling me again, so I counted them as lucky. After the court proceedings, they were found guilty and sentenced to be hung by the neck until dead. The execution was to be set immediately after the trial.

Damian and Dan stood there looking at their once captors and lovers, Tim and Jason, thinking about the tender moments they had once shared only days earlier. Now they have to hang them alongside those memories. Damian looked at Dan and said, "I thought it could be love." Dan replied, "So did I." Damian looked at Dan again and said, I'm so sorry, you were always the only one who truly loved me. I could always tell when I looked into your eyes. I saw myself as you saw me; for the love, I gave you reflected right back. And when you give me that big passionate bear hug every night, it was a moment of euphoric bliss.

Snap! Tim and Jason's bodies twitched as they slowly lost consciousness and died. That was it. All the riders headed back to the plantation as night soon approached. When Dan and Damian finally arrived home, they were greeted by their father sitting on the front porch. This was very unusual. When the boys met with him, he said, "Daniel, Damian... We have a problem that we need to address. Apparently, Tim and Jason loved to be involved with women too. Three of our field workers are pregnant, and they all have claimed that one of the two are the fathers. Well, I have just been informed that both of them are dead, so let's just let nature take its course. Problem solved."

Chapter IV

THE NEW PHOENIX

In Egyptian mythology, the phoenix was said to bear scarlet and golden feathers and was as large as an eagle. It is said that there can only be one phoenix in the world at any one time, and when a phoenix was approaching its death, it would construct a nest of scented branches and spices and would burst into flames to which a new phoenix would rise from his ashes.

ichael and I were in our room just horsing around, doing nothing in particular, which is nice for a change, when he looked at me and paused. He told me that something recently came up about us being so affectionate and how much we enjoyed each other's company. Michael had heard via a few sources that some of the workers were commenting about us.

I asked, "Should we be concerned?"

"First of all, we stand out in any crowd we are in. One devilishly handsome black guy with one not so bad looking Kentucky boy, we make a rather sexy couple. From here on out, everything between us is becoming far more obvious, especially in North

Carolina. But my love, I do want to begin by telling you that I am in no way concerned about this plantation. Those farmworkers/slaves you see, they work for me. I know I have not told you this, but my father is Mr. Jackson, and he sees to it that I'm very well taken care of, educated, and I have input into the operation of this plantation. My twin brothers are fully aware of all this. I have avoided playing the plantation card."

"I wanted you to love me for who I am and not for what I have. I love you as you, Jim, just a simple cowboy from Kentucky. I just wanted you to love me for me. I wanted our relationship to blossom filled with love, compassion, understanding and forgiveness. Also, you are the most rugged and handsome white man I've ever met in my life, if I may say so."

With the absence of Tim and Jason, the house felt a bit drearier. We discontinued our nightly dinners and went back to three nights a week. With each dinner, the atmosphere was very relaxed, and a multitude of subjects, including farming, personal, etc. was discussed without any negativity or discrimination. It was a refreshing turn of pace that helped raise morale for the entire family and plantation alike.

In the ending months of 1862, we had possibly the worst winter that the plantation has ever experienced in

North Carolina. The temperatures frequently fell well below the low teens and snow, sleet, rain, and what felt like just about every other element of nature came in at full force. The only two rooms that we could keep warm were Michael's private quarters and the quarters that Tim and Dan occupied when they were together. Mr. Jackson stayed with Michael and me, while Dan and Damian remained in the Big House in their quarters.

Mr. Jackson complained that the Big House was indeed too big too properly heat with just a fireplace alone and that the twins shared the master bedroom with the only other fireplace located in the house. But he enjoyed spending nights filled with company in his waning days. That night, something magical happened. Damian was sleeping in the same bed that he and Jason had shared. That once special magic that was sparked in his relationship with Jason now suddenly ignited with Dan. They had spent many nights together and experienced just about everything that can be experienced between two men, but that night Damian and Dan's lovemaking was beyond each other's expectations. They had reached a new level in their relationship, and with that newfound energy, they felt confident that they could handle any obstacle that came their way.

In mid-December of 1862, Mr. Jackson came down with a heavy chest cold. Every day it seemed to worsen, and his temperature continued to climb as he became frailer. Michael reviewed all of his medical books and determined that Mr. Jackson was suffering from an acute case of pneumonia. There was no known cure for pneumonia only treating it with hot compresses, lots of liquids and lots of rest. Michael felt that all of these treatments could be handled at the plantation. He personally saw to it that a room at the big house was properly set up just as if it was a hospital room and had two portable fireplaces rushed in from Charleston. Mr. Jackson was transferred from Michael's clinic to the big house, and a private nurse watched him around the clock.

By the first of January 1863, Mr. Jackson was at a point where we had his private minister say a prayer for him. Shortly after that, he passed away and was buried in the private cemetery on the estate. 1863 was a disastrous year for all of us in the South. Lincoln decreed the Emancipation Proclamation on January 1, which meant that all of the slaves were now free. We have 600 acres and had 100 slaves, but without them, our operation would cease to exist. In the coming days, a new plantation operation would be born.

At the end of February, there were only twenty-three farmworkers currently left. The majority of them were household staff and mostly elderly. Eight were farmhands that were used to work the crops. Damian began to calculate with the current staff on hand, along with his brothers and me, what crops that we should plant and harvest to get us the greatest return on our labor per acre investment. We all sat back in amazement. Where did you learn all this? Well, I guess my relationship with Jason didn't go to waste; let's see if this works.

We decided to go right along with Damian's plan, and if it did work out as he projected, we would be able to keep the plantation solvent for the entire season. With Mr. Jackson now gone, it was just the four of us that met for dinner. Our depth of conversation was kind of shallow without Mr. Jackson. We spent more time talking about relationships and communication with each other than we did the farm and business. I thought it was nice that we could do that; it kept our little family close. Many families miss that opportunity. That's where love should be, and you don't want to miss it.

As of early 1863, the plantation had been spared by any invasion from enemy forces. All of us had been planning for it and preparing a safe place to hide our valuables like art, silver and items that we could not replace. When the raids seemingly were over, and the Union troops were pushed out of the region, things went back to whatever normal we now have to live by. In fact, the whole year went by, and everything and everyone was now stuck in this new normal.

Never letting their guard down, the plantation had periodic drills in preparation for the arrival of enemy forces. Everyone had a place to go and knew where food and water were located for when that fateful day comes, and we knew that day would come. One day one of our field hands came running into the barn extremely exhausted, sweat pouring down his face and barely coherent. He told me that there was a cloud of smoke coming in our direction, and as far as he knew, there was nobody out on our acreage today. I immediately sounded the alarm to activate our escape procedure. I was the only one authorized to stay behind and present myself as an out of luck cowboy who stumbled upon on this place and was hiding out here until I get ready to go someplace else.

Five Union troops arrived on horseback with torches in hand and asked me who I was, where I was from, and what I was doing here. Of course, I gave them my story, but they still wanted to check the property out to make sure it was cleared. I told them that I already checked for anything valuable, but I wasn't the first person to ransack this home, so I just wanted to save you the search for there are only a few loaves of bread left, but they are hard as a rock.

One of the troops started to dismount his horse and peek inside the dark rooms. I recognized who was in charge and threw him half a hard loaf; he looked at the other troops and said the bread had to be at least three or more weeks old, this place isn't worth it. I sold it. They ended up riding off into the sunset. Before they did, they did, however, inquire as to the other plantations in the general area, and I told him that I didn't stop or investigate any other ones; this was my first find on my travels south.

When I gave the signal that it was all over, Michael came running at me, grabbed me, and hauled my ass to the barn. He said, "I knew that I was in love with this dumb ass cowboy from Kentucky, but honey, you scared the shit out of me today! It took me twenty-seven years to find you and rest assured that I am never giving you up without a fight!" Then we made love as if that was our last time and stayed tangled up in each other's arms until we were awakened by those damn roosters the next morning.

Rubbed & scrubbed, I was feeling and smelling good. I left the bathroom refreshed and headed straight for the big house for breakfast. As usual, the four of us discussed our daily plans, but unlike most days, we were lucky, for Michael was able to work on the plantation for most of the day. Dan and Damian, however, would be stuck tending to the fields all day, so they wouldn't have the chance to spend time with their brother. As for me, the cattle and updating the fencing usually is a full-day event. I kept track of all my fencing builds on the plot maps I created and built them segment by segment to help advance my build times.

Today, Michael was running the plantation since everyone else was out of the house. I was walking past the barn when suddenly, I was yanked into the barn and then slammed onto the wall. Before I could even get my wits about me, my lips were locked in one of the deepest kisses I had ever received. "Jesus, Michael! Don't scare me like that!" He laughed and said, "See, I can be the rough one as well," as he grabbed hold of me and led me into the stables where I saddled him.

Michael told me afterward that he had this terrible feeling that he was never going to see me again, that it seemed so real and overpowering, and if it was the case, he did not want to regret a single thing and take pleasure in my embrace.

"I have the same fears sometimes myself; the only difference is that you are here on the plantation today, Michael. This is probably the safest place to be in town, and you are next to the man who will keep us as safe as we can be, I promise. I'll tell you what I'm going to do; I'm going to instruct the foreman to leave a guard in the barn for when I'm not here, is that okay with you?"

Michael responded, "Sure, that would be fine; in fact, I could use one to run errands around the compound, which would save me a great deal of time."

The next day was like any other day. We all were out doing our daily routine when around two o'clock in the afternoon, the alarm bell began to ring. Everybody knew where to go, but I was out in the woods trying my hand at bagging me a buck with my rife, so I was oblivious to what was going on. Michael began to panic and knew that the only person who was authorized to talk to any adversary was me, but I was gone.

Then what appeared to be soldiers were now marching into the plantation's drive. Michael decided that he would represent my position in this encounter. The union soldiers rode up, and the first thing out of the captain's mouth was, "Who owns this plantation?" Michael replied, "I do." The captain snarled, "Can you prove it."

"Of course; please follow me." They entered the big house and proceeded to Mr. Jackson's old office, where Michael went to some filing cabinets and pulled out the deed to the property. The deed was in the name of Damian, Dan and Michael. All three of the last names the same. The captain said, "I need to see all three owners." Michael replied that he would send a field hand to locate them and bring them back as soon as possible, but it could take two to three hours.

The captain became irate and wanted proof that Michael was who he said he was. He told Michael that any black person could say something as preposterous as this, so what makes this statement true? Michael returned to the filing cabinet and came back with his birth certificate, showing his date and time of birth, name, his father's name, his mother's name and a small image of his footprint. The captain didn't buy it. Things began to escalate rapidly.

Michael began to flee to the back door, and two of the house servants blocked passage of the soldiers that were chasing them. At this time, I had been watching the situation unfold from behind some trees, rifle locked on the two soldiers pursuing Michael. Fortunately enough, the servants were able to allow Michael to escape as I signaled to him to head my way, and we ran to one of the designated hiding places. That night the big house was ravaged, and all the buildings and homes were torched. Virtually nothing was left standing of the plantation. The only good news was that all of the staff were safe, and so was the cache of the most cherished and valued possessions that we had hidden. Michael had managed the plantation through this crisis as best as he could and was enormously proud of himself, for no one was killed even though he was sad at the loss of his father's house.

When the men returned that night and found the plantation completely destroyed, needless to say, they were beyond angry. They immediately wanted to pursue the soldiers and seek revenge. Michael explained to them that there's far too many, they probably numbered in the 20s or so, that it would be a suicide mission. Damian and Dan were not so easily convinced. They said that those soldiers destroyed the only home that they've ever known and violated the memory of their father. Revenge was a must. Within an hour, Damian, Dan, our foremen and I were armed and ready to pursue the soldiers. Michael was going to stay at the plantation as he and the remaining staff set up a makeshift infirmary with a fortification in case we have to come in riding hot.

Our plantation only covered a few acres north, so traveling at night was not going to be an easy task. To the northern soldier's disadvantage, they did not account for anyone following them, and twenty soldiers leave enough tracks that even a blind man could follow them. Now the problem would be following them at night, but me being from Kentucky, I learned how to track at an early age, so day or night, it did not matter to me. We were going to catch them! We discovered that the northerners had set up camp early, not straying too far from our plantation. It didn't appear that they weren't anticipating any attack because no guards were posted, and all of them seemed to be heading to sleep.

Now we set forth to develop our plan of attack. I had been in many battles over the last two years and gave a scenario that gave us the best odds that victory. I told everyone that we were almost at a total disadvantage for they were trained soldiers and had the experience and numbers to their benefit, so the element of surprise would be our best tool. Damian and Dan each took two foremen while I took only one and created a group to encircle the compound. Next, we needed to find the commanding officer, which we did by locating the unit's flag posted outside his tent. I covered that position because I was that accurate of a shot, and I also learned in battle when the leader falls, the followers panic. So, we wanted to send them into disarray.

All four groups had the encampment surrounded; I was designated as the one who would eliminate the captain in the command tent. I was fortunate because it was located on the outside perimeter of the encampment with no guards posted. I took my pistols and knife and proceeded to the tent as one of the foremen watched over me with his rifle. When I entered, I found the captain and his lieutenant both fast asleep. Now I had to strategize how to eliminate them both without waking the entire regiment. First, I muzzled the captain's and slit his throat then as the lieutenant began to stir around, I quickly stabbed him in the heart while covering his mouth, watching the life fade from his eyes. The captain, still gargling on blood and holding his throat, looked upon me with utter fear in his eyes. I slowly raised up, and he tried to reach for his pistol, but I quickly stepped on his arm and jammed my blade so hard through his windpipe that his neck was severed, instantly killing him. I left the tent and returned to my post on the west side of the compound. I signaled to Damian and Dan along with the foremen the all-clear sign, and we readied ourselves for the battle.

We waited until daybreak, and the regiment began to stir, and mourning reveille was being prepared. A soldier entered the command tent and immediately exited with a yell warning all troops that the commander and the Lieutenant were killed. The regiment was put on full alert, and confusion set in as to who was in command. As they formed in a close circle in camp, I signaled to begin firing on them. Within ten minutes, we had killed approximately fifteen of the northern troops. There were only two or three left scattered around the encampment. We remained in our positions, well undercover until the remainder of the regiment was executed.

It wasn't too long that we return to the plantation and found Michael organizing the gatehouse, which was not destroyed with the plantation. The gatehouse had a long history because it was used as a temporary residence during the construction of the big house. Michael ran over and hugged me and asked what happened. I told him that only two foremen were injured during our battle, but we took care of things. Michael said, well, it looks like everyone is going to be living together in the gatehouse until further arrangements can be made. The gatehouse was not all that fancy; it had one bedroom, a small living room, kitchen with a small stable attached to it big enough for four horses. This is going to be a new adventure for us because we have never lived together before.

Michael partitioned off the one bedroom with a sheet so all of us could have our privacy, as little as we could muster at least. The first night Michael and I curled up together and made love as if there was no one in the room but us. I had survived the fight with the union soldiers, and coming home to Michael was my greatest gift. Despite all of the horrors of the past few days, our love only grew deeper. We knew that whatever our future might bring that it was going to take hard work and great planning to get back to where we had been before.

Damian and Dan were closer than we have ever seen. We had never shared a bedroom with them before, so we did not know what to expect. Michael and I always thought that Damian would be the aggressor, and Dan would be passive, but we were surprised to hear Dan dominating Damian in bed! We could tell all the action just by the pleasurable moans that Damian yelled out during the night. Michael told me that the weeks ahead were going to be a new learning experience for all of us, as new plans had to be made to restore life to our plantation.

Chapter V

THE CITY THAT CARE FORGOT

The city of New Orleans, with its laid-back nature and somewhat lawless lifestyle, was the birthplace of modern poker and craps. And until the mid-20th century, New Orleans had more miles of canals than Venice, Italy.

After a couple of months, we realized that the plantation would never be restored to its former glory or even to a level where it would be productive enough to be self-sufficient. Michael and I made plans to leave and go further south, possibly towards New Orleans. Damian and Dan were going to stay behind in an attempt to find a buyer for the land and then join us in New Orleans at a later date.

As soon as we made it to New Orleans, we decided to rent a small bungalow just on the outskirts of the black part of town, the Faubourg Treme. A few days passed, and Michael received a job in a medical office at a hospital that served near the area. As for me, since I'm just a cowhand from Kentucky who happens to know how to shoot a gun, I still was pondering my options. I decided to apply at the local Sheriff's office just for kicks, and to my surprise, I was hired as a deputy on the spot.

We couldn't be happier, as for myself, coming from Kentucky growing up on a farm, not knowing really how everything in the world runs, the big city was all new to me. But I had Michael. I have fallen in love with the most precious person in the world, and I wanted to give him everything that I am and have. I am a woman for a man and a man when the time comes. I feel as if I'm possibly the most blessed and spoiled lover in history. Tender and fulfilling, his love has given me the most unimaginable relationship far past anything that I could ever imagine.

In about six months, we received a message from Damian informing us that the plantation has been sold, and they only needed Michael's signature, and the sales price would be enough to keep us all comfortable for the rest of our lives. As soon as all the papers are signed, they would be joining us in New Orleans. Michael and I rejoiced to hear the good news. A messenger was dispatched immediately to our house, and upon arrival, he witnessed Michael's endorsement and took the paperwork back to Damian, who then proceeded with the sale.

New Orleans is such a wondrously vibrant city, nothing like I had ever experienced before. There are hundreds of remarkable structures, festive celebrations, and excellent places to eat! Due to that last fact, it had taken us a while to decide on a place to dine. Our final decision was this French restaurant down in the heart of the French quarter. It had received rave reviews from the locals we conversed with, so we decided to give it a try. When we entered the restaurant the maître d' immediately asked if we had a reservation and of course our answer was no we don't. He then told us that they would not have a table available tonight and that he was terribly sorry. I was rather curious about how this restaurant could be sold out when there were so many empty tables around. His direct answer was, "We do not serve Negroes in this restaurant, sir."

Well, the candle was ignited. I held up my badge and identified myself and requested the presence of the owner, who eventually showed up. I attempted to inform the owner that it was against the law to discriminate now due to the Reconstruction Act, but my attempts went in vain. Michael grabbed my arm and dragged me out of there. He said, "Jim, we're too good for that place, and you are too good of a man. Thank you, my love, for defending me, but let's go somewhere coffee and crème can stir together." We both started to laugh. We stopped at the first open place. I don't remember exactly where we went, because we both ended up becoming distinctly inebriated. Now the nightlife was something that I will never forget. It was indeed a night of splendor, and each night somehow was always better than the night before.

April 4, 1864, four months have passed now, and Damian and Dan arrived bearing gifts for all and started looking for a property that would be befitting the Jackson name. Of course, we were going to partner up, so a single-family ranch, farm or cattle operation is what we were looking for. They were working with two or three different land brokers, and the conversation always seemed to get around to, "Where are you two from again, and you two really act different." Other than the fact they were almost identical twins and at times dressed accordingly, in my opinion, it takes one to know one.

Everything was going wonderfully. Damian and Dan had purchased a cattle operation consisting of 700 acres, and Michael was enjoying his position at the hospital. And I can happily say that I was using my skills and talent to my fullest potential by out-shooting, out-punching and out-drinking anyone in town. As a deputy, I felt that I was bringing some form of justice to the world, but at night when I was alone with Michael, I was able to break all the laws… with butt sex.

Lately, I have been receiving an alarming number of complaints from various ranchers, that small herds of cattle were being stolen on the nearby ranches. That night after I told Michael about the allegations, I said that I would ride out to the ranch the next morning and warn Damian and Dan. The following day as I approached the ranch, I heard gunshots coming from the west side of the ranch. I quickly took out my pistol and sprinted towards the back of the house. In approaching the area where I heard the shots ring out, I saw Dan in full pursuit of two riders. One rider stopped, took out his rifle and shot Dan dead center in the chest.

When I reached Dan, he was slumped over in the saddle; the shot looked as if it pierced his heart, killing him instantly. I took him off his stead and laid his body on the ground, checking his vitals, praying for a miracle. He was dead. When I looked up, I could see Damian riding in from a distance. I wondered how I should handle telling Damian that Dan was dead. I was so nervous because I had never been in a position like this before. When Damian got there, I just walked up to him and put my arms around him and started to cry. He put his arms around me and said, "Is Dan... is my brother dead?" Damian began to cry hysterically and, with great rage, tried to struggle to get to his horse to ride out after his brother's murderers. I grabbed Damian with both hands around his neck, pulling him in close to me, shouting, "Damian! Damian! Listen to me! I know how you feel! But riding out there right now is a death sentence! This is not like the plantation; we do not know the lay of the land, and that man executed a shot that even put shivers down my spine! Rushing after them with no rifles or back up is a march to suicide."

He stopped struggling, and with a shaky voice, he whimpered, "Jim... he's gone." Damian dropped to his knees; his eyes swelled with tears once more as a distant expression filled his face. I embraced him once more and just held him.

We had a white granite mausoleum constructed for Dan on a private cemetery and held a small, intimate ceremony in his honor. Michael and I spent the entire day with Damian knowing that he was heartbroken and completely distraught. When nightfall came, we headed back to town, leaving Damian to his own accord. The next afternoon we came back and found him drunk and in the same clothes that he was in the day before. He said I don't know how I can live without my lover. Michael and I did not have an answer for him, only that we knew that time is what Damian needed to overcome the loss of Dan.

We decided to alternate our visits to the ranch to check up on Damian and always found him in a state of depression. Whiskey tainted his breath, seeping out his pores and staining every garment of clothing he ever touched. And with each visit, he seemed to have gotten worse. The ranch had not been attended to. The house had become cluttered and messy; clothes were scattered about. This was not like Damian, to say the least. When Michael traveled back to his medical office, he researched depression, attempting to find a medication that would help his brother. Michael discussed with me that Native Americans had a solution to his crippling depression in the form of "loco grass." We knew that was not truly a solution but just a temporary hold on his state of mind.

As the weeks slowly grew into months, we realized that Damian could not stay on the ranch alone. We convinced him it was time to sell his property and move to town with us and try to start a new life. Michael and I purchased a larger home in an upscale section of New

Orleans with the funds we received from the selling of the plantation. There we had four bedrooms, a living room, dining room, three bathrooms and a beautiful kitchen. Damian sold the ranch along with the cattle and was filthy rich. He didn't need to worry about working, so we made it his responsibility to look after the house. It was almost like living at the plantation. All of the precious silver and antiques from the plantation had been brought to our new house. Damian had it all decked out with memories of our past, so each night, when we got together, it was like going home.

My typical day was patrolling by horseback in the rough parts of town. The city was already full of vice, but these parts were flooded with people drinking on the streets, prostitution, unsanctioned duels, fights and just filth. I was assigned to that area because of my particular talent with a gun and my redneck spirit of Kentucky, which made me fearless but not foolish. One day when I was riding down the street, I heard a familiar voice call out, "Jim." I looked around, and there stood Kevin, one of my two friends from Kentucky, that I had lost track of during the war. He was excited to see me and couldn't wait to shake my hand. He asked what happened to me, what was going on in my life, and where I was living today. I didn't know how to answer his questions. I was caught in a trap I would have to either lie my way out or face up to the truths. Kevin and I were remarkably close when we were younger but never sexually. I knew of his sexual conquests that he emphatically bragged about, but I never met any of them or got involved in any detailed conversations. We had kept our private lives discreet.

Kevin wasted no time in inquiring about my living arrangements in New Orleans. He wanted to know all about how I got here, where I was staying, and what happened to me. I was trying to wrap my hand around all of the questions and trying to formulate an answer that would make sense. I thought for a minute and decided to take a risk and invited him to dinner that night. I rode over to the hospital where Michael was. I told him what had transpired and that I invited Kevin to dinner tonight. I apologized for not clearing it with him at first, for I was put on the spot and asked him how he felt about my decision. He told me that it was okay and that I better hurry and get home to tell Damian were having dinner guests tonight so he can cook up something special.

Kevin arrived promptly at seven o'clock. To my surprise, he was not shocked by the lavishness of our home nor of the occupants. During dinner, the four of us were completely engaged in casual conversations about the war, the loss of the plantation and Michael being a doctor. I then introduced Michael as my partner. Kevin was not surprised but rather delighted. He said that the only thing that genuinely surprised him was the fact that I had found such a remarkable individual who was so well polished, educated and pleasantly attractive to love. He said he always thought of me as a rough old redneck but had a sneaking suspicion that I might have had a higher sexual attraction towards men than women. He had no qualm over my sexuality because he had messed around with men before and never told me.

Our conversation drug on until the late night, so we invited him to sleep over instead of going back to his seedy hotel room. Kevin was a real gem, but as with most men from Kentucky, he was unpolished. He stood six feet and had a slender build. His chestnut brown hair was closely cropped, and his beard was neatly trimmed. He had all the physical appearances of a dashingly gorgeous man. That night Damian took great care into getting Kevin's room ready for the night. Michael and I noticed that this was the first time that Damian had shown any interest in another person since Dan's passing.

As time lingered on, Kevin continued joining us for nightly dinners. The four of us have become very comfortable with each other, and we talked about various topics, including relationships with other men. Damian finally felt a sense of comfort and told Kevin about his twin brother Dan, with whom he had a relationship for years and how he had been murdered on their ranch by cattle rustlers a few months ago. Kevin was very understanding of Damian's loss and outwardly showed affection towards him whenever possible. During dinner one night, Damian bashfully asked Kevin if he cared to move in with them instead of living in a hotel. With glee in his eyes, Kevin grabbing both of Damian's hands with his own and fervidly jumped at the opportunity. I saw the sparkle coming back in Damian's eyes that was once there when he was with Dan. Kevin's arrival seemed to be a blessing, and now the four of us could proceed happily with our lives.

Damian and Kevin's relationship took a while to blossom. There was no rush, and Kevin understood Damian's fragility. I helped Kevin obtain a job as a deputy sheriff, as it was a better match for his skill set than the previous position he held before as a cargo clerk for a local shipping company. Damian continued to take care of the house and decided to bring in the former cook from the plantation to help prepare our meals. As you remember, the cook was actually Michael's mother, and he was incredibly happy to have her back in the household. She was also delighted with Michael's relationship with me and to see Damian coming back to life again. She grew fond of Kevin and his simple way of life and would trade idioms that they knew constantly.

One night, Kevin came home rather late and missed dinner. When he arrived in his room, Damian met him by the bed, overly concerned. Kevin explained to him that he had an extremely grueling day, was covered with grime and stunk to high heaven. All he wanted was a hot soothing bath with lavender and chamomile and then to eat. Damian was quick to draw him a hot tub so that Kevin could soak and recharge his batteries. After he had finished, he walked into his bedroom with his towel wrapped around him, and Damian was sitting on his bed. Both of them looked at each other, wondering who would make the first move.

Kevin dropped his towels to the floor and stood there naked in front of Damian, gleaming. The longer Kevin stood there, the more engorged his penis got. Soon Damian got up from the bed walked bewitchingly towards Kevin, putting his soft, firm arms around him and locked lips with him slightly biting his bottom lip and pulling it back playfully. Kevin put his hands around Damian's waist, pulling him close and delicately whispering into his ear, "I guess I have to go through you to get to dinner," and pushed Damian roughly back on the bed. His penis was fairly erect now and ready to take charge. He unbuttoned Damian's shirt smelling his slightly sweet cologne. He then slowly removed his pants, not knowing what to expect. When Damian was fully unclothed, he displayed a gorgeous crop of blonde pubic hair and an uncut erect penis of substantial size. Kevin was taken aback by Damian's beauty and could not resist ravishing his body for the first time. Damian laid back on the bed, submissive to his core, and allowed Kevin to take whatever pleasures he desired from his body.

Kevin started with the toes and worked his way up his legs and then to his hairy balls and dick. He slowed his approach to his chest, twirling his tongue around his nipples and then finally moved up to his neck and lips, taking great pleasure in both. It was not long before Kevin flipped Damian over on his stomach, and he proceeded to take pleasure in his manhole. Damian moaned with pleasure as Kevin drove it home. They both climaxed simultaneously. That night they slept arm in arm together in Kevin's room for the very first time. After that, they would routinely switch off between both of their rooms for their nightly encounters, which in time developed into a very loving relationship. With Damian now emotionally mended, we continued our four lives with a new sense of normalcy, at least for the time being.

Regarding Michael, I have said it many times before, but he is genuinely an exceptional individual. His work ethic was beyond anything that I have ever seen before, dedicating multiple hours a day, every day reading the medical books of new and old as well as dabbling in the field of chemistry. Due to all his first-class efforts and vast knowledge, his hospital promoted him to the chief medical officer, and his duties were expanded to include social fundraisers and awareness programs. In my position as a deputy sheriff, I, too, had become incredibly popular and well known in the community. During one of many hosted events, the Sheriff stopped by to inform me of his plans for retiring. He stressed to me that he was getting a little too old to keep up with the hustle and bustle of the city and wished to go back up north to enjoy the more peaceful life of the country.

He sat me down and expressed that out of his thirty years of service, he had not once met a deputy as exemplary as me and that I should run for Sheriff.

He smiled and said, "You're the talk of the town. I think hands down you're going to win this election; you by far are the best man for the job. and you have my full support."

After a brief run for the Sheriff's office, I won unanimously and celebrated with Michael that night on the town. At dinner, Michael gave me this beautiful dark cherrywood box; the box alone was a present itself. I opened the box, and to my surprise was a pair of custom-designed Cooper Pocket Double Action revolvers. I just looked at Michael with amazement as he said to me with a beautiful smile, "I can't have my Sherriff going out ill-equipped, now can I?" He knew exactly how to make a Kentucky boy cry. Now that Michael is one of the heads of the hospital, and I was sheriff of New Orleans, we were in our infancy to becoming one of New Orleans's new "Power Couples."

Soon we found ourselves hosting a plethora of dinner parties at our home. Whenever we did host a function, Damian and Kevin would use the side entrance to enter the house, having dinner in the kitchen so as not to interrupt our proceedings and then make their way up to their private quarters. There was that lingering question that seems to pop up at most of our gatherings. "Where are the ladies of the house?"

If that was not the exact statement, then something very similar to it was always uttered. We firmly stated to all our guests and colleagues that we were both confirmed bachelors and business partners who met on Michael's plantation several years ago. That, in a way, I owe Michael a life debt, for he had saved me after a battle. But we are determined in every way, to keep things as un-confusing and simple as we could and to put our fortunes first.

Kevin excelled as a deputy. Like me, he was such a redneck at work that no one would ever suspect that he was such a lady in bed. Damian was flourishing as well. He added additional servants since our bed linens needed to be laundered and changed daily, of course. The added social events required extra hands. And sometimes all four of us could not make it to dinner at the same time, so we needed staff to ensure that dinner preparations would be arranged according to each of our schedules.

Michael and I gradually became more visible in social circles, and our influence in New Orleans had grown to a level that we were almost recognized everywhere we went. Our social gatherings grew larger and, of course, more complicated to maintain. The day after one of our charity events, we all were sitting at the table having breakfast, and I brought up a concern about how all of our social activities were interfering with the Damian and Kevin's private lives. I told everyone that we should buy another house large enough to hold all of these events at the same time and close enough that the four of us could share dinners like we used to do on the plantation. Three or four nights a week max, just so that we can keep up with each other and talk about what's going on around town. All warmly welcomed the idea, and Damian offered to buy our current house at market value and give us a small bonus as a thank you for all that we had done to help him throughout the years. Michael told him that wasn't necessary -- that they were brothers. But Damian wouldn't have any of it and uncharacteristically, put his foot down similar to their father, the late Mr. Jackson.

I suggested to Michael that he should be the one to complete the house search seeing that he is the one with all the money, and I'm sure that I will agree with his selection. So, within three weeks, Michael had composed a listing of five large houses that met all our needs, but out of those five, he decided that we should take a gander at only two of them. The first manor we looked at was nearly identical in layout to our home on the plantation -- beautiful white pillars and a double entry door leading into the grand entry with circular twin staircases. It contained five bedrooms and three baths, all located on the top floor while the lower level held two additional bedrooms, the living room, parlor, dining room, a large French themed kitchen attached to the servant's quarters, and two large multi-toilet bathrooms for guests. This house was huge, and it was sold fully furnished, and the furnishings were antique and fit the house to a Tee.

The second home we looked at was not as stately. It had a two-story build, but it lacked a front porch with the pillars we so coveted. On each side of the main building, there was a one-story structure that merged into the house, giving it a unique multi-level appeal. When entering the main door made of solid oak, you immediately walked ahead to see a single circular stairway that led to only four bedrooms and two baths. On the lower level on the right side of the main structure was an extensive, well-maintained library, with what seemed to have a vast amount of academic literature on just about any subject that you could dream of. On the left side of the main structure, there was an extra-large living room that could convert easily into a mid-sized ballroom. The dining rooms entrance was elegantly placed under the stairway, and walking in was a beauty to behold for the high ceilings paired with the large arched windows let in a lot of light, giving the room a unique sense of open grandeur. The full brick kitchen, along with a traditional large brick oven was built behind the living room and connected to the dining room.

As we discussed both houses, we determined that even though gorgeous as it was, the second house was not nearly big or grand enough for us to host our parties. We ultimately settled on purchasing the first manner. Michael handled all the paperwork, and he put the property in both our names and then proceeded to finish with the closing. That night at dinner, we told the guys that we had purchased a home and that we would be moving within the next two weeks. Damian was first to suggest going over and take a look at our new place so he can help properly furnish it. He asked Michael if he would like to bring over some of the items from the plantation. Michael told Damian that the house had already come completely furnished and that the furnishings were quite adequate.

"But what's the harm in going over there together and taking a look, my dear brother. After all, you know there is no eye better than Damian's when it comes to decoration," I chimed in.

Within three weeks, Michael and I were all moved in and were now in the process of hiring new servants. Michael asked me since I actively met people throughout town as Sheriff if I knew any good people that would be willing to work. He stressed that the most critical factor was that they needed to be individuals that we could trust whole-heartedly. That day I met with Kevin and told him that Michael and I were looking for servants for our new home and that if he by chance stumbled across a well-mannered family or two on his patrol to give me a heads up, and upon his recommendation, I would love to have a word with them. A few days passed, and Kevin had a list of four suitable families and their addresses who were ready for my interview. I thanked him for his recommendation and began to study the list of names.

I went back to the headquarters and ran their names through the records we had on file, and nothing appeared. I then looked on the wall map to pinpoint their addresses and marked them to research what neighborhood they lived in and how close they were to the property. I then allocated enough time for the next two days to make appointments with the following families and met with them. I had various positions that needed to be filled and wanted to enlist the help of a particular class of men to serve as our valets. Now you know the old saying, "It takes one to know one." You could say that I used this saying to search for new employees.

By the end of the second day, I had come up with the finalized list of names and positions. I decided to hire a total of eight exceptional people. Two went by the names Jered and Antwon, who were assigned as our own personal valets. Jared was eighteen years old from a mixed creole heritage who was fairly light of skin and tall. Antwon was as black as black can get. He was twenty years of age and stood approximately 6'3". Michael referred to Antwon as the boogieman for at night all you would be able to see is a pair of eyes followed by a dazzling white smile that would float around the manor like a rhythmic ghost scaring Michael, which only corroborated the stories of how haunted New Orleans really is in his mind. I, on the other hand, couldn't find anything more beautiful than his deep black walnut skin, well, other than Michael's, of course. So, in the end, Michael eventually took Jared, and I was awarded Antwon.

I hired a rather spectacular man in his mid-30s by the name of Marcos to be the sole butler for the manor. Marcos had the innate ability to be there exactly when we needed him and not a second more. In a way, he was our information network and security, for he tapped into the network of servants around New Orleans far and wide and gathered little tidbits, all the while covering his tracks and protecting our names. One would think that Marcos was born a seasoned spy due to his mystical nature, but the man had an unwavering loyalty that you could only read about. The five other hires were relatively attractive women, but more than that, they were extremely tight-lipped. Their primary duties were to work the laundry room, the kitchen, and to take care of the housekeeping.

Michael and I had never had a valet before, so this was virgin territory for us. We had to determine what was on and off-limits with the staff since we were so used to living so close together naturally. I asked Michael if we should meet with them formally and set some ground rules? Michael nodded slightly and said that it was an excellent idea; the sooner, the better.

Two nights later, Michael and I met with Antwon and Jared in our dining room. We asked them if there was anything that we had done that possibly put them at unease with their positions? They were not surprised by the question. Antwon was the first one to speak out saying, "Whatever you both do between yourselves is first and foremost not any of our concern, but to be honest with you it doesn't bother us at all because Jared and I do the same thing you're doing behind your back in a way."

Jared jubilantly chimed in, "Well, it looks like we are all in this together, so let's enjoy!" Michael shot him a sharp look, which set him back in line. "Do you need anything else, sir?"

We held the first cocktail party in our new house as an open event in support of our new medical Center at the hospital. The majority of the people in attendance tonight would be the top 1% of New Orleans. Michael did not tell me that staggering percentage; I think the less I knew about things like that, the better off I would be. The reception was fully staffed by our valets, the butler, and six women, including Michael's mother in the kitchen.

Then came the time of the night that Michael, master of ceremonies, had to go on center stage and make a series of prearranged announcements. He recognized all of the top 1% of New Orleans as they dropped their donation check in the fishbowl by the podium. As one of the individuals approached the podium to deposit his check, he turned around and asked the crowd, "Let's see the contribution of the 'power couple' of New Orleans."

Now Michael's wit took over and said, "Well, come now; I'm not foolish enough to pretend that I am akin to the top 1%, but... I do not know this about Jim. He is here tonight, so I will let him speak for himself." As I was rambling to the stage, trying to think of something humorous to say, all that came to mind was, "Ladies and Gentlemen, this, what you see here, is all I've ever been my entire life. A rancher, a gun hand, a farmhand, and now Sheriff. And what I have to show can be seen on the ledgers at the First National Bank downtown."

The crowd gave a resounding round of applause. The evening grew to an end, and the party was over. Michael and I looked at each other, and we shared but only one comment between the two of us. "I love you."

The next morning, we were alone in the kitchen, having breakfast. I told Michael that it was about time for him to hire a personal assistant due to his ever-increasing workload. It has begun to affect our home life, and he couldn't possibly keep up that pace forever. I told him that I was genuinely concerned about his health, and sometimes it's the people around you who will see it first before you do, and seldom do they realize their overall effect on others.

I told Michael that Kevin had more than enough qualifications to compile a list of well-suited professionals to interview for the assistants' position, someone who can help him out with all the nonmedical issues. Michael said, go ahead and let's see what happens, but please make sure they could at the very least be fluent in both English and French—ending with the warm, mellow chuckle that he always had.

Kevin gave me the list; I went through the process of interviewing each candidate, and I came up with three prospects for Michael to interview. All three were from higher class families and had been well-educated in private schools. All three were looking for a job that had good future potential, and all were multi-lingual. I thought that any of them could fill the position adequately; however, I told Michael that it would come down to his personal preference.

After meeting with each candidate and further scrutinizing each of their applications, Michael finally decided to hire the twenty-year-old French man by the name of Justin Beaumont. Justin stood 6'1", slender build, his face bared every pre-shaved whisker along his jawline, and handsomely dressed in a fully tailored dark gray suit. You could see your face on the toe of his highly polished shoe, and he walked with the grace of a swan. Justin was an individual that you only had to tell something once, and he did it. He was on top of the daily calendar and had Michael organized and fully briefed before every meeting that he attended. Justin was an amazing individual; in a way, reminded me of Jason, dare I say?

Michael came home from work a lot earlier now, so much so that we resumed our weekly dinners with Damian and Kevin. Their house was in immaculate order, and they keep an incredibly low profile in the town. They rarely had guests over; we were the only guests that they had over for quite some time. Michael and I treasured this newfound time alone. We had side-by-side bedrooms with entry doors between us, so one night, we would use his bed, the next mine. Our valets doubled as our personal assistants, knew to change the sheets in both rooms and reminded everyone that it was nobody else's business what went on in our bedrooms. We have grown to be quite comfortable with our valets, maybe too comfortable. The next morning when I was taking a shower, Antwon was now standing there ready with a towel. My body still glistening from the water, as I came out, he gave me a slight nod and handed me my towel to cover my naked frame. It was quite apparent that his eyes were examining my entire body; I did not like this. I talked to Michael about this, and he said the same things were happening with Jared. He felt that it was time that we spoke with the boys.

The very next morning, we had a meeting with Jared and Antwon. We made sure both of them understood that Michael and I were in a lifelong monogamous relationship and utterly devoted to one another. We took every opportunity to eliminate people from our lives that did not wish the best for our relationship. We firmly stated that if they want to continue working as our valets, they would have to adjust their desire to have a four-way sexual encounter with us immediately because it would never happen. Michael and I did not care what they did between each other, but we did care about how they conducted themselves in the performance of their duties and how they were representing this house.

It seemed as though our conversation with them sunk in, and they returned to a thoroughly professional relationship with us. Michael and I felt at ease again and continued with our lives. Justin, Michael's assistant, was playing a more significant role in Michael's life every day. Michael turned over more and more duties to him, which he accomplished without hesitation. One evening over dinner, Michael brought up the fact that he would like to invite Justin over. He asked if the next time we had one of our social galas, would it be okay if he invited Justin. I said, "Of course! He is probably the one who is going to arrange it all in the first place, so it would be nice for him to see the results of his organization skills."

It was about two weeks later that we hosted a small dinner party for eight elites in New Orleans. Altogether, including Justin, there were eleven in total in attendance for our party. Michael and I watched as Justin conversed intellectually with the other attendees at the dinner party. We were so impressed that he was so at ease with these elite individuals as if they were old friends. After everyone had gone, we asked him why he was so comfortable with these individuals.

"Well, they're from my part of town." Little did we know that the private boarding school that he went to taught some of the wealthiest family's children in New Orleans as well. Michael and I were overly impressed. Justin became a permanent fixture at all of our functions from then on. He added a spark of youth and exuberance that we lacked.

Additionally, he drew the attention away from us and towards himself. After every event, he would go around and shake people's hands and thank them for their attendance and that he would be in touch with them for future events. He left no doubt in their mind that he was the one that organized Michael's events.

The elite of New Orleans now focused their energy on Justin as the right person to know at the medical center, to stay on top of the social event calendar.

Periodically, we would invite Justin to join the four of us for dinner at one of our weekly get-togethers. In the beginning, we were concerned about how he would react to our obvious relationships. But when he did join us for dinner, he gave no indication or concern that anything was other than just as it should be. It was rather refreshing. The best part about Justin was that he just simply never changed how he interacted with Michael, on any level, at their office or off the clock.

During the next few months, Justin joined us several times at our residence for dinner. One thing that we did notice was that Jared and Antwon were making a noticeable fuss over him. Justin did not seem to respond to their outward flirtations, so we didn't think much about it. We talked to Jared and Antwon about their interactions with Justin, and they asked Michael and me about his personal life and where he was from. We just informed them that we did not know anything about his personal life other than he was a highly educated individual who went to a private school with some of the children of the wealthiest families in New Orleans. We left it at that.

One day when Michael came home from work, he told me that Justin had said to him that Antwon had approached him after work and asked if he would like to join Jared and him for some drinks sometime. Michael said that Justin did not seem to be particularly interested and had politely refused. One night when we were having dinner alone, I asked Antwon what he had talked with Justin about that other day. I told him that we particularly did not want the two of them to be involved with Justin because they were now getting involved in my professional life, and this was simply unacceptable.

Antwon reacted somewhat aggressively, "What I do on my time off is not any of your concern, and I would never bring any form of shame into this household under any circumstance. Jared and I value our relationship with you and Jim, unconditionally. So, I just want you to know that if we are interested in Justin, it is only to enhance further the relationship that we already have. Jared and I can tell that Justin enjoys being a part of this family, so why not let him?"

Michael and I thought about Antwon's comment and knew full well that Justin was not going to be a part of our family in the way Damian and Kevin were. The bonds of trust could only stretch so far for an outsider. The four of us formed a family based on love, and we look out for one another and are there for each other without fail. This responsibility is not going to be shared with anyone else in the world, not even Justin, as wonderful as he may be.

Not surprisingly, Jared and Antwon continued to pursue Justin until, eventually, they were able to convince him to join them for an evening of social drinking. From then on, their relationship grew faster than anyone could imagine. Justin did not have any hesitations about interacting with people below his class level. He found Jared and Antwon sexually appealing and fun to be around. He was able to be less formal, and let's say, 'able to let his hair down' when he was around them, which he enjoyed.

All three of them had unique living situations. Justin lived at his parent's home while Jared and Antwon shared a bedroom upstairs at Michael and Jim's manner. Each of them desired to be emancipated from their current living arrangements and wanted the freedom that comes with living on one's own. The three of them concluded that they each wanted to live by the rules they set, so they began discussing a plan for a possibly more open future for them all.

At our next evening meal, Justin joined us. After the last plate was cleared and all cups finally dried, we all decided to call it a night and excused ourselves from the table for the evening was done. Justin jumped up from his chair, clearing his throat, and addressed us all, saying that he was going to stay around and help Jared and Antwon finished their duties because they were going out for a drink tonight. Michael and I were astounded to hear this. This was the first time that we heard Justin admit to any involvement with Jared and Antwon.

"Okay, well, you be safe out there and good night." After we said goodbye, Michael and I went to our rooms and noticed that our clothes had been laid out for the next day, in both bedrooms, of course. Both beds were turned down, and the table lamp right next to the bed was lit. Our valets had apparently planned ahead and completed their tasks ahead of schedule.

Antwon was the mastermind of the evening. He had the Butler sleep in his and Jared's bedroom. After they finished cleaning up after dinner, Antwon suggested the three of them go to the butler's bedroom for a nightcap. They entered his bedroom, poured each other a drink, and Jared and Antwon sat on the bed while Justin sat on the chair. An awkward silence had befallen the room, and everyone just sipped their drinks thinking, now what? It was Justin who initially broke the ice. He said without shame, "I have fantasized about a three-way with you two for such a long time now, so… what are we waiting for?

No time was wasted. Shirts, pants, socks, underwear flew every in direction. Soon all three were huddled in a mass in the middle of the Butler's bed. For the first ten minutes, there was nothing but looking and feeling going on. All three were in amazement as to each other's beauty. Then the first passionate kiss came, followed by all three lips meeting at one time. Their bodies were perfect for each other, so lean and smooth. Each of their endowments was beyond belief.

Now the confusion set in. What to do to who and when? They were bonded entirely from the very start and wanted to share the intimacy that engorged them equally amongst each other. They continued playing and satisfying each other's every wonder till the morning sun rose.

Everything was going wonderfully in all of our lives. Justin's work for Michael at the office had not changed; it only got better with time. Michael's coming home early. Our life together was a storybook of love. The only thing that seemed to have changed over time was that Justin was now joining the four of us for dinner more often. And of course, Michael and I discussed that very topic. Michael said that it would be best if he talked to Justin.

"I will find out the extent of things when he comes to dinner tomorrow," Michael said, "for I am curious who is continuously inviting him to dinner because I know it's not me? And I know Justin has enough sense not to just show up to his employer's house uninvited."

The next day when he met with Justin, he asked that very question. Justin replied, "Generally, Antwon invites me."

"Justin, have you ever given thought that it is unusual for a house servant to invite a guest to dinner?" Justin gave it some thought and said, "Michael, it seems to me that all six of you are family. I felt that the invitation coming from Antwon came from you, too. You all are one, so I felt that if Antwon invited me to dinner, then you all wished me to come. I apologize for my misunderstanding."

Michael said, "Thank you, Justin, that will be all. We will talk later." Michael looked down at his desk in a total state of bewilderment. I guess over the years, Jared and Antwon have together become who they represent. I guess I have to understand that someone who valets and acts as their acting personal assistant for so long, and so intimately, can't help but to know about every move his representative makes.

When Michael shred his discussion with Justin with me, I was amazed at how quickly I understood how everything could have happened. It was an animal instinct. If you want to get close to your prey, you blend in and copy them or their surroundings. I wondered if that applied in this case. I am not one to trust anyone except Michael and Damian. I am always looking for wolves in sheep clothing and trying to make sure that the four of us stay vigilant for any betrayals, for we all are power players in this city, and all could have potential targets on our backs.

One night, when Michael and I were having a nice quiet dinner at home, Antwon walked up to me and stood erect. He said, "Mr. Jackson, may I ask you a question?" I looked up at him and said, "Sure."

Antwon said, "I would like to know if it would be okay if Justin moved into this house?" His immediate response was, "Jim and I will have to discuss this, and I will get back to you."

Oh, what a discussion we had. Michael and I were not surprised, but having Justin move in here was pushing all of the boundaries. Michael said, "There are so many negatives for him being here. Not only do we, the power couple of New Orleans, live here, but if the chief medical officer's assistant also lives together with them, there will be questions going about, and we don't need that."

We needed to come to a solution and fast. The only answer we could come up with was that the three of them get their own apartment together, close by so that when Jared and Antwon got off of work, they could still be close to home. Justin is well compensated, and we can look into making some type of financial arrangement for Jared and Antwon to make all of this work out if they want to.

We met with them the next morning before work and discussed our plan for them, and they agreed to it. They were able to quickly find a small house located behind a mansion not far from us. We knew the owners as they were one of our houseguests for various functions. So, we were able to vouch for them and to secure the rental agreement without making a deposit. The rent we divided by three, and each individual was responsible for their share. In our case, we gave Jared and Antwon a monthly stipend to pay their rent. We also incorporated it into their contract that this monthly stipend would only occur while they work for us. Within days they had moved into their new home.

All three of them had similar tastes in decoration and furniture styles, which made designing the new home a fun and adventurous experience. They enjoyed the same type of meals and also enjoyed cooking for each other. Frankly, as time passed, they found that there was less and less that differentiated them from each other. Even during sex, which by the way, was unusually outstanding, they did not know what role they were going to play until they played it. They were universally made for each other.

Justin's responsibilities grew at the hospital once again. Now he had taken on human resources responsible for the administrative division of the hospital. This was in addition to being the assistant to the chief medical officer. Even with these increased responsibilities, his assistance to Michael never faltered. He treated him as if he was God, and at the same time made the world believe it. Each function that he organized and coordinated was to make Michael look even more impressive than he was. That was his goal. And so far, so good.

Damian and Kevin have been extremely happy together. Kevin's job has become more challenging in the last few months. He covers Jim's old areas, plus an additional rough neighborhood in the black part of town. He's in the saddle hours at work; his work shift grew from six to eight hours a day. He was explaining all this to Damian, not to justify his sometimes more stressed moods, but just letting him know that he has no control over what happens at work. He said that he does not want to play favorites with Jim to get him to pull some strings to change things. He already felt indebted to Jim as it was and tried to show him that he was every bit of the man Jim said he was and refused to run from any hardships.

Damian calmly replied to him, "Then what are brothers for?" Family is family; we take care of our own. If one falls into hardship, then we all fall into hardship. It is our prime directive, our obligated duty to each other to lift another when they have stumbled, and we have never left any man behind that we embraced as a brother, a lover, our kin. And we shall never do it now. So, satisfy your anxieties and relinquish your sense of pride; we operate as a team, and this team wants all its members to be successful, for we are all we have. That is what we have always done, and this is what we will do again.

The next day Damian got in touch with me. He went over the discussion that he and Kevin had the night before and that Kevin was not bitching about it.

He was merely explaining to him why he was coming home tired, late, and sometimes mentally on edge from work. "I personally think that his work schedule should be adjusted; everybody deserves a good quality of life, don't they?" Damian stated.

I was thinking back when I practically did the same thing for Michael by getting him an assistant. I thought maybe I should take a look at the number of deputies in that precinct and see how I could better utilize my resources without overstressing my staff, not just Kevin. I did an in-depth analysis of each precinct in my jurisdiction; redrew patrol blocks to maximize the efficiency of my officers, like the ones Kevin was working. After a thorough comparison, I set up command units for grouped areas, changed the tactics we used in each district with more emphasis on service style policing across the board. It was more of a watchman approach in areas of higher crime. We accepted that vice was just the very nature of this city but tasked a special unit to take down the more hardened enterprises.

This unit employed our best and toughest, spearheaded by Kevin. The group was to take a more legalistic approach to police policies. The job came with more danger but with better pay and more downtime, which I knew he would appreciate. When the restructuring began, I heard that his precinct was short two deputies in comparison to all the others. So, I notified the precinct commander that he was authorized to hire two new deputies as soon as possible. I told Kevin that when we swear in the additional deputies, we could officially give a title to your new unit.

"You can finally take a break and let some of your deputies take the lead. The precinct commander told me he owed you a great deal of gratitude for always picking up any of our men's slack, so thank you, you earned this promotion."

I did not mention anything about the conversation I had with Damian, and we had our nightly dinners as a family as usual. It was about six weeks when, finally, a discussion occurred about Kevin's well-being. With a grin from ear to ear, Damian told us that Kevin was coming home in better spirits now and had far more vigor than he ever had seen him have before. Kevin went on to explain that on top of hiring two more men, his new position heading the county's new task force was exciting. He could see the difference he does in this city almost instantaneously. Damian did, however, say that his workday was reduced back to six hours a day, which gave him far more time to spend at home. He continued saying that with that amount of time, it gave him enough rest, meal breaks, and the opportunity to meet the citizens we are helping.

And Damian added, "It is sure nice having him home before six o'clock at night. We sure do enjoy our evenings together."

It was Monday morning, and Michael was in his office. It was well past nine o'clock, and Justin was always promptly there before eight, like clockwork. It was highly unusual for him to be late even by five minutes. Michael sent an intern to the big house to speak to Antwon about Justin's presence this morning at home. Antwon told the intern that he was there this morning when he and Jared left for work at six. He generally leaves sometime after seven since he works at eight. Antwon explained that no one was at their house right now, but the people in the owner's home were still there, so maybe you could ask them if they have seen Justin.

Michael knew the owners but did not want to get them involved; the less they knew about what was going on, the better. Michael came to my office around lunch. I told him to explain everything to me and that I could have one of my deputies' ride over and check to see if Justin was at his house. I told him I would take care of it right away. Shortly after, I received a report that no one was there, and the house was ransacked. I sent a deputy to pick up Michael, and we immediately returned home. We discussed our findings with Antwon and Jared, and they had no idea what would justify what the police had found. I said that the four of us should go there and check things out.

When we got there, it was evident to me that the room was deliberately tossed around, and whoever did this had no intention of looking for anything; they just wanted to make it look like somebody was looking for something. Pointblank, it was staged. I shared my opinion with everyone.

I told them we need to figure out why and who staged it. Well, it did not take long, for when we got home, a messenger from Michael's office was waiting for us. He said that the hospital's secretary had received an envelope marked urgent, immediate reply necessary and it was lying on his desk. Michael and I headed to his office immediately. Inside was a poorly written ransom letter demanding $20,000 for the safe return of Justin or the queer life of the "power couple," and their family would be widely distributed all over the state of Louisiana.

This has to be a conspiracy we said; no one person would know that much about us to write this unless they knew us, we thought. Jared, Antwon and Justin are all involved in this caper now. All we need to do is get to the bottom of this. I called my headquarters to have two deputies go to my house and arrest Jared and Antwon and take them to headquarters and put them in separate cells in isolation until I got there. This is the only way I knew that I could control their communication until I had a chance to talk to them.

When I got back to the station, I met with Antwon first, because he is always the one who plots everything and carries out all schemes. I came right out and explained to him every part of this scheme that we discovered and the ransom letter that Michael had received. I also told him that he will never return to the big house and that his job and all benefits have been canceled as of today. Michael and I are confident that in some way, large or small, you and Jared played a role in this. I just sat there silently and waited for a reply.

Antwon admitted that Justin had been asking all kinds of questions about Michael and I's private life. Antwon thought that he just had a sexual fantasy like he once had and was getting off on just hearing about you guys. Never at any time did Jared or I have any suspicion that Justin was going to blackmail us by trying to discredit our family. I was taken aback by his use of family and us. After just being fired, he was still addressing himself as family.

Next, I talked to Jared. I went through the same dissertation as I did with Antwon, but Jared was not as strong. He started crying and just could not understand why Justin would ever do that to them. He told me that they both loved him and cared for him a great deal. He said, "I guess that we got suckered into telling too much about you and Michael, but we never, not in a million years thought that he would use that against us. I decided that both Jared and Antwon were not involved in this predicament and gave them their positions back on the condition that they return to the big house and report any sightings of Justin directly to me.

I sent a deputy to talk to Michael to tell him what I had found. He explained to him that it appeared that Justin was the mastermind behind this whole operation and that I would be home later to explain more about our predicament. Damian, Kevin, Michael and I all got together at our house, and we started to strategize how to handle the situation. $20,000 is a lot of money. Is our personal life worth that much? We have substantial wealth and, in a worst-case scenario, could live out the rest of our days in comfort without worrying about a job. The only thing different that could affect us now was our possible fall from grace. Damian and Kevin have kept a low profile throughout the years. Few people, outside our circle of friends, know them as a couple, so the impact on them would be insignificant. Now for Michael and me, the "Power Couple" of New Orleans, who have been so visible and well-known by the majority of the city, that fall from grace would come as a crushing blow.

We looked at each other, and I said we had been together for five years now, and it seemed like only yesterday that I met you. Since we met, all aspects of my life have been an adventure, and there is nothing out there that we cannot handle together. So, we both agreed to let Justin's offer expire. We had no concern for Justin or about the publishing of the Power Couple's sex life. We would take our chances. Three weeks after the deadline, there was no press or notification of any kind that concerned us, so we were wondered if this whole situation was going just to die a quiet death. Little did we know that the finishing touches were being made on the publication of the "Golden Couple Sex Lives" and was hitting newsstands tomorrow.

Tomorrow came, and on the cover of all three major papers, about twelve full columns in length and not a single detail missed in the description of the love life of the "Golden Couple." All four of us were amazed as to the specific details that the writer gave to describe our private lives. Well now, we had to prepare ourselves for the massive influx of letters and or doorknockers. Michael and I went back to our particular offices. My office was a little more protected, and since I am the town's sheriff, I was not too approachable, to begin with.

That night on the way home, I was stopped by one of my next-door neighbors. He had read the article and wanted to let me know that the neighborhood had no problem or concern with the article. He said that if everything was true that I still had his support. I thanked him for his understanding and returned home.

For the next month, we had peaks and valleys. Michael endured the most humiliation; I came along a distant second. Damian and Kevin avoided the majority of the fallout and went on with their lives as usual. As Sheriff, I was an elected official, so my public perception and support are invaluable. I was making every effort to make myself more visible to the public and to shake as many hands as I can before the next election. I was determined not to lose this election simply due to my sexuality.

With election day approaching, the mud started to fly. My opponent, one of my deputies, was a real red neck! He habitually used the word 'faggot' as much as possible in every speech. My rebuttal to any question about my relationship was, "Yes, I have a partner." I did not blink an eye when I made the statement, and I meant it from the bottom of my heart. Some may have questioned me, but they couldn't question the results that I produced and my love for Michael.

During one of our town meetings, a group of protestors began to clamor in the back, yelling that I wasn't fit to hold my position, that what I was doing was against both God and the righteousness of this great city and office. They challenged me, saying that I was the sole reason for the bastardization of our once-great police force and how could anyone trust a faggot to carry out the law. The two men with the loudest voices were the pastor of my rival's church and a man who I had seen somewhere but couldn't put my finger on where. They both tried to rile up the audience against me.

The mystery man would constantly interrupt everyone on stage, and I respectfully told him that I wouldn't take this level of disrespect anymore and that I'd have one of my deputies escort him outside. He replied, "The hell I'm going to be told what to do by some God damn faggot! You are not fit to wear that badge, and I will take it off you one way or another!" That was a direct challenge to me.

I chuckled, "So... City Park at three o'clock sharp. I'm going to shoot you dead." I pointed at him, and the crowd grew silent. City Park was a popular meeting place to hold duels, and any questions about my competency would end there.

After the meeting, I immediately went down to the park, where a large group had gathered. I saw the pastor and several of the faces of the dissenters in the crowd. The pastor introduced himself and said that he would bear witness to this event announcing me as the sheriff as of now and motioned to the mystery man to introduce himself.

The man looked at me to speak when I immediately cut him off, saying, "I have no use for the name of a dead man. Give it to the tomb maker with a message that reads: here lies the decimated corpse of a man foolish enough to challenge one of the twelve Demons of the South. I'll have the good pastor pick up what's left of you and put it in a box."

It was one minute before the hour; we had lined up -- our signal would be the bell towers chime when it hit three o'clock. We stared at each other, pistols in our holsters when suddenly I heard the clock go "Dong," and with a swift clean pull, I fired directly from the hip. He fired, but I could tell that my shot hit him first, because his pistol leaned to the side slightly, and his face squinted up slightly. His shot missed as he fell backward on his rear. As my right as the victor, my opponent's life was at my mercy. Dueling etiquette also permitted me to desecrate the body as I chose. I walked up to him, pistol in my hand as he began to cry, begging me for his life, that Mitch, the deputy who I was running against, put him up to this and that he was sorry. Before he could utter another word, I sent one last round between his eyes, knocking his head back as I continued walking on past his body, never losing a step in my stride.

I turned around and addressed the crowd, "Does anyone else have any doubt in my abilities to administer law and order in my town? Pastor! Do you have a few words to say?" He quickly shook his head no. I glanced around to a muted crowd; every mouth shut as if they were sealed hermetically. I turned and walked away. Everyone got my point. I returned home; my shirt speckled with blood. Michael saw me and immediately rushed over to me, asking if I was injured. I told him that I was not and what had happened. He was furious with what I told him I had done. He said, "Why in the world would you put yourself in harm's way like that! You could have died! Why didn't you immediately come and get me? What could you possibly gain from the way you handled things?"

I responded in a calming tone, "I knew that you would try to stop me if I told you. No matter what I have done in the past, most people would still question me due to my sexuality. The only thing I could do is re-establish their faith as the one person in this world that you never want to cross. I have nothing to hide and no one to fear."

Michael let out a sigh and said, "Well, I guess we won't be getting any shit from now on." I laughed, and he kissed me on my forehead and told me to wash up; dinner was about to be served. In my new life, honesty is the best policy. This deceptive game that I have played for so many years can now thankfully be laid to rest.

The next day I rose to a different world in a way. People knew me but now feared me as well. The talk about my sexual identity all but evaporated then. It was a bit strange being so feared on the streets where I was once so loved and admired. Tensions started to fade as people saw that I was still the same person I always was, and the only people who needed to fear me were those who wished the people or me malicious intent. With the election day rapidly approaching, I felt more confident in my standings as sheriff than ever before.

Chapter VI

THE RISE OF THE SHERIFF

The term shire reeve first appeared on England around the early 11ᵗʰ century, when William the Conqueror defeated England replacing the great Anglo-Saxon Earldoms with the sheriff. The sheriff became the direct representation of the king in his county and held court to punish minor offenders. Later a reduction of his power led to the sheriff only being able to arrest and imprison criminals. In 1829, the first modern police force was established in London, England.

*W*hen all the votes were counted, I was elected Sheriff by an overwhelming margin. Twenty plus percent lead, read the newspaper. Michael and I celebrated on the podium together, and I thanked the entire town for their support and understanding. On our walk home that night, we put our arms around each other for the first time on the streets in New Orleans. A new day had come at least for the city of New Orleans. I returned to my job as Sheriff the next day, just as if nothing had ever changed. Everybody was doing their same job; everything was the same as yesterday except today they have a gay Sheriff. Now I wondered if I was going to encounter any new challenges.

The first item that I noticed was the daily crime rate report. There seemed to be more reported crimes in the area of town frequented by gays than there was before. I did a little research and discovered that for months before my re-election, there was never a report out of that section of town. So, at the next commander's meeting, I brought up the fact that I had noticed an uptick in crime in the area known to be frequented by homosexuals. I asked if someone could give me an explanation for this increase.

One of the aged commanders stood up and said, "I am sure you understand the unwritten code that we always take care of our own." I was a bit confused as to what he meant by that and said, "Are you saying that now that we have a gay Sheriff, we should give special protection to his community to show respect for him. Correct? Is that what I'm understanding?"

"Well, maybe I can clear this up," he said, "Today we are a part of them, and they are a part of us. Yesterday, they were not a part of us, and we were not a part of them, so we did not take care of them. Within your department, we have every nationality, and until yesterday we never had an openly gay police officer. So now they are a part of us, and we are part of them, do you understand?"

Until today, I did not know we had our own nationality. Ha-Ha. I just returned to my office and sat down and thought for a few moments about my newfound position in life—the Gay Sheriff. I was wondering if all of my Kentucky redneck-ways had prepared me for this. Well, I guess they did because I turned out to be a rather butch gay Sheriff. It was something I was incredibly grateful for because I did not have to do anything differently. I did not have to change my walk, my talk, or the way I hung my pistols. I have always been this way; it was incredible.

I told Michael about my realization of my position, and then asked him how he was managing at work? Michael said everything was flowing perfectly; one of the secretaries stepped up and filled Justin's position, and she was doing an excellent job. He said he did not have to do as many social events to generate the same amount of cash donations as before, so everything was going well, just fewer social pressures.

"Speaking of Justin, whatever became of the man?" Michael inquired. I told him that he skipped town the day of his disappearance, and after that whole failed extortion scheme, he sullied not only his name but his family's name as well. My men lost track of him when he fled Baton Rouge. Michael looked at me with saddened eyes and said, "It's such a shame that we constantly are betrayed by those we welcomed in with open arms." I held his hand and said, "Yes, but we will always have each other, for my heart belongs to you just as surely as the moon belongs to the night sky."

Life in the city was beginning to become mundane for all of us, at our various dinner gatherings. We began discussing plantation life and the quality of life we had when we lived on our father's land, running our own operation. The more we discussed it, the more all of us grew nostalgic and started to wonder how we could turn our idea from just conversation to something we could breathe life into. We designated Damian and Kevin to search for plantations that would meet our standards. I arranged for an unpaid leave of absence for Kevin so that he could join Damian in the property search. Within hours Damian and Kevin were meeting the local land brokers to identify potential plantations.

Four days later, Damian and Kevin contacted us and told us that they decided on two properties, and we needed to take a look at them. We agreed to meet that night for dinner at our house so we could discuss their plans in more detail. That night Damian talked about the first plantation. It was described as very grand; beautiful grounds, 400 acres, adequate barns, and additional housing for farmworkers. It came partially furnished, and our furnishings would complement the place.

Kevin described the second property. He said it was 900 acres of prime real estate—more than adequate barns and stables, farmworkers housings, and a large spring-fed pond. The main house left a little to be desired. It was not up to our usual standard of living. It had three bedrooms and only two bathrooms. There are no servants' quarters, and the largest room of the house is the dining room. Now our only hope was that Damian would be able to use his magic touch on that property to make it livable. I cannot overemphasize that it was an absolute steal.

The next day we took the time to visit both properties. Kevin was so right in his description of the main house; Damian would have to use three magic wands to make that into a frilly home for us city queens. Damian's description of his property was right on. The main house was absolutely beautiful, and one that truly met our standards, and the barns and various outbuildings were as described. Now Kevin walked out on the ranchland and pointed out that there was no water, no real tillable land, all this acreage is suitable for our cattle at best. If cattle and horses were both grazing this small pasture together, there would not be enough grass, and we would have to supplement it with hay, which is another cost factor. Kevin said, "I always try to look at things like, where am I going to get the best return for my investment?"

All of us had the information now and our own opinions. We decided to have dinner tonight at our house to discuss our property options. We went through all the pros and cons of the properties and said that we would sleep on it for the night. The next morning at breakfast, we all decided to support Kevin's proposal for the second property. The first house is a home but would not give a return on investment. The land and water of the second property are the returns of investment. And the price was so low that it didn't even make a dent in our checkbook. Michael and Damian continued to handle the paperwork; Michael put me on the deed, but Damian did not put Kevin. I didn't know precisely what that signified, but it is a good feeling to know that Michael trusts me. I never had any doubt, nor should anyone doubt my love for Michael.

That night Michael and I were having a quiet dinner and discussing how long it would take to move both homes to that little house on the plantation? He thought that we should think about doing some construction on the house before we moved in to expand and improve the structures.

"That's a great idea; we can get that mess out of the way while we are not living there," I confirmed with Michael. No sooner did we start talking about the new plantation, Antwon showed up in his usual inquisitive manner. "What is this about moving? What are you going to do with us?"

I replied, "There's no problem; there are three bedrooms, and you're coming too, but I'm sure there's going to be some changes in duties. Antwon was relieved and spread the word to Jared that they were moving to a plantation this summer.

Three months passed, and Michael and Damian had supervised construction on the main house to expand the living room and parlor rooms, build a library, add four servants' quarters with five additional large bedrooms & bathrooms. In addition, they built a private medical section for Michael so that he could re-establish his medical practice in the community. Everyone was ready to move. We decided that Damian and Kevin would move in first as they possessed most of the family heirlooms.

We would move in last, only taking absolutely necessary items. We were planning to sell our house fully furnished, similar to what it was originally. Damian and Kevin's possessions more than adequately filled the house, they looked stunning. The only thing Michael and I would need to bring were our personal possessions. We left it up to Antwon and Jared to ensure that all of our own items were properly moved to the new house.

For Michael and me, our interest in our jobs started to fade. It was a fifty-minute ride to town for both of us, so I left at eight in the morning and got to work about nine. I usually left at four, so I could be home by five at the latest. Every day of work seemed so mundane compared to when I was home, breathing the fresh air and doing something constructive at the plantation. It seemed as if every night at dinner, we would discuss our future departure from our current jobs, planning what time would be right for us.

The time has finally come. Over dinner, the four of us agreed that the end of my term as Sheriff would be our final work date. This was a little over three months away. We talked about how time had flown by, how Michael and I met in 1862, and about our plans for today, the eve of 1870.

For eight years, we had shared true love and happiness without a curse word or an argument. Michael had to be the kindest, most gentle soul that I have ever met. Sometimes I wondered why I deserved such an individual. I was always concerned about Kevin's feelings when there were, at times, obvious signs of family disconnection. As an outsider myself, I felt comfortable talking to him about it.

Before the next time, the four of us had dinner together, I met with Kevin and discussed the issue of family connection. He was very understanding. Kevin just simply stated that he came here with nothing, he has received more love than he ever imagined in a lifetime and if he left here with nothing, he would still be a winner. I could sure relate to that, so I thanked him for his honesty and wished him a good night.

Once a month, Jared and Antwon received the same overnight pass. This past week they had asked if it was okay to extend their pass for two days spanning Tuesday and Wednesday. I okayed it, and they said that they would be staying Tuesday night off of the plantation and return Thursday morning at six o'clock for their regular shifts. Well, it was now Friday morning. Neither Jared nor Antwon had returned from their weekend. I decided to contact the Sheriff to file a missing person's case. With my influence, as well as my former position, an all-points bulletin was dispatched to all area police officials.

Within two hours, the body of a savagely beaten black man was found in the alley in the poor black area of town. He was taken to the same hospital that Michael used to work for observations and treatment. I arrived at the crime scene about fifteen minutes after it was reported. As I scanned the crime scene, I zeroed in on a red handkerchief. I then remembered something I saw at our morning breakfast. Antwon and Jared both had on blue slacks, white shirts, with a red bandana draping out of their right pocket. Could this be one of theirs? I had to find out what hospital did the authorities take this person of interest to. The officer in charge was new and could not differentiate me from your average citizen on the street.

I told him to summon a more senior officer in his detail. He refused, said that he was in control of this investigation, needed no lip from a bystander, and I should just move along. In the meantime, several people had gathered on the street, and a couple in the crowd recognized me. I walked up and asked them for their help. I told them that two dear friends of mine had been injured or killed, and their bodies have been moved. It is my understanding that one of them went to the hospital, would any of them by chance know which hospital it is? One woman spoke up and said the one near the black ward. I immediately asked if there was anybody in the crowd that was traveling to or by River Road? To my surprise, there was.

I asked them if they could pass on a letter to Michael on our plantation, for it was of the utmost importance. They agreed to do so and said that they would leave immediately and for me to rest assure for they would get the letter delivered for me. I thanked them kindly and continued my inquiry with the people around, hoping to find any additional clues. My letter made it to Michael before the hour's end. I told him about all of my findings and that either Jared or Antwon was at his former hospital, and I didn't find out any more information. I asked him if there was something that he can do to help me and that I will be waiting near the hospital for a response.

He immediately picked up a pen and began writing down a bunch of information and crafted a second letter telling the current hospital director about the situation at hand and to check for any persons by the name of Jared or Antwon Jefferson. Michael gave the man the two letters with a handsome reward for delivery and said to him to tell me that he would be there within the hour and that the patient would come under his personal supervision.

It took thirty-six hours before we were able to question the patient who we now know for sure was Antwon. The Sheriff and I agreed that we would let Michael handle the line of questioning.

Michael calmly said to Antwon, "Slowly and as accurately as you can, walk us through what you remember the night you and Jared were attacked." He said, "They were three men brandishing lead pipes. One of them worked Jared over, and the other two came after me. The last I saw of Jared, he was lying flat out on the pavement, not moving. They continued to beat on me until I blacked out. They had bags over their heads, but I managed to look at their hands, and two of them white and one was black."

One thing he could not shake was how unusually frail one of the white guys was. He asked about Jared, and I told him that we still did not have any leads to where he may be.

Within the week, Jared's body was discovered about two miles outside of town along the riverbank, beaten to a pulp and his head bashed in. His right orbital was so damaged that his eye hung outside of it. I barely recognized him by his red handkerchief hanging out of his right pocket and a scar he obtained from working as our valet. I had the local photographer take pictures of his body for evidence documenting the brutality of the crime.

I said to an old colleague who was assigned to the case that when we capture these individuals, and we will, I want to see to it that they receive the maximum punishment under the law. We postpone Jared's funeral until Antwon was out of the hospital and fully recovered. He was the first family member to be laid to rest on our new plantation. Michael took care of the necessary paperwork to make Jared officially a Jackson after his death. So maybe Jared's legacy can be lived on through Antwon.

I hired two more individuals to take Jared and Antwon's old positions. Now that Antwon was officially part of the family, he would have more responsibilities and would be seated at the table when it comes to decision-making. He would be served by staff and receive his own room. The new valets that we hired, William and Bobby, were doing an exceptionally good job taking over for Antwon and Jared. We trained them from the very start on the rules and regulations of our private life and what was considered off-limit areas of our home when either Michael or I was home alone. I conferred with them that they would have to share a bedroom that connected with Antwon's.

On their last day of training, I told them the severity of our non-interference rule with any of the family members and that it would be truly wise for them to mind their manners. William and Bobby bowed their heads and took off to their room. William was an eighteen-year-old male who stood about 5'7" with a smooth, slender build. Bobby was about the same age, 5'8", and also exhibited a slim build but was more athletically toned. Both men had a deep dark mahogany complexion, short black curly hair, and cleanly shaven from head to toe.

The plantation was running ever so smoothly. Our family and staff were in full swing. Seeing Damian and Kevin work was a sight to behold for you had never seen redneck cowboys so gay, but yet so diligent. And for Michael and me? We were more deeply in love than each day before.

The Sheriff's office received a letter from a town about 460 miles away in Georgia. They had detained three individuals matching the description of our wanted posters, and they wanted to know if we wanted them to be brought over for questioning. The Sheriff met with me, discussing the transfer, and I told him that we would appreciate it if it happened as soon as possible. After a brief re-deputization, Kevin and I received permission to head out there and bring back the detainees who would thus be in Kevin's custody. He, however, gave one caveat; he also wanted to send an extra deputy with us to make sure everything was handled properly, and no grudges were taken out unlawfully. It took us four long days of riding, but on the fourth day late one evening, we arrived in Fayetteville to transport the prisoners. I asked Kevin to go to the hotel and secure three rooms, and the deputy and I would go to the jail to identify the prisoners. Not to my surprise, one of the white guys was Justin. The other two were just thugs that Justin was leading around. I looked at Justin with disgust and immediately turned around and headed over to the hotel.

I was exhausted after four days on the trail, but seeing his face energized me with a hatred that was set to explode if I did not calm myself promptly. I arranged for a hot bath, ate a poorly prepared meal, and slept the night away. The next morning, all three of us met for breakfast at 7:00 AM and made plans for a five to six-day return trip because it wouldn't be nearly as strenuous as the trip here. We needed to be well-rested and on guard because of our prisoners.

During our long trip home, Justin's lips became loose. He started with one story then proceeded into another story that led to another story of how he needed help in his life because he felt so unloved. Michael was the only person in the world he ever loved, and he could never get in between Michael or me, so he ended up feeling so unimaginably unloved and unwanted. All he wanted was for Michael to feel as much pain and suffering as he had, so he could know how much he had hurt him. And these last two attempts were designed to do just that. I thought to myself, 'Well, wait till his story hits the front page of the newspapers, that is if he lives long enough to tell his story that is.' Luckily this time, we live on a plantation, so the fallout will not be the same as last time.

Justin's trial lasted almost two weeks. His defense team brought in a handful of individuals who testified as to their relationship with Michael. Michael's attorney provided the court a list of his witnesses. The defense attorney immediately objected, stating that all on the list were either hired help or family members, and none of the testimonies could be relied upon. Justin's attorney recommended that they should be removed from the witness list because they would not be impartial. The judge agreed. At that very moment, Michael had no one to represent him.

That night in bed, with our arms around each other, Michael looked at me and said, "What am I going to do?" I told him that public opinion is with us. We are or have been the power couple of New Orleans for a considerable amount of time, and his medical service to the community is well known. My reputation as Sheriff goes without question, and Justin is an imposter who disgraced not just himself but also his family and now is charged with murder. We have nothing to worry about. We had amazing sex that night, and Michael dominated me with his love, and I surrendered every redneck bone in my body.

When the jury came in, Justin was found guilty of murder in the first degree. He was sentenced to be hung by the neck until dead. The other two men were also to be tried for murder separately. Within a few days, they were also found guilty of murder in the first degree. Within the week, all three men were hung and were now history in our lives. Neither the city nor any of our friends raised an eyebrow as to the information the trial revealed. Our life went on as usual at the plantation. Nearly a whole year has gone by, and It was almost the end of 1871. Together now for almost a decade, Michael and I have experienced many of the highs and lows of love. It had, indeed, been a fantastic journey.

January 1, 1872, arrived without much fanfare. This was the first New Year's Day that Michael and I were able to be together alone in a few years. We decided to meet Damian and Kevin for lunch today at a small bistro on the south side of town. We had reservations, so we were in no rush to beat the lines, so Michael and I enjoyed our ride there, embracing each other in our carriage, kissing one another gently while admiring each other's beauty.

At one o'clock, we arrived for lunch with a healthy appetite. When inside, we were shown to our table where Damian and Kevin were already waiting. We greeted each other as usual and began talking about our respective days. The whole time we all chatted, Damian was awfully quiet; I had thought to myself that something must be on his mind. After we all finished our first glass of wine, Kevin brought up the fact that he was not happy in his relationship anymore.

Damian said, "Our love has faded since we moved to the plantation. It seems as though there is a city boy inside of me wanting something different. I know you're uncomfortable doing your duties in front of another person, so we need to work things out. This is a message that I sent Antwon, and I hope that you agree to our way of life here."

No fingers were pointed. Michael and I looked at each other, not knowing what to say. Michael spoke up and said, "Damian, what do you do is up to you. You are family; this should be your decision alone."

He said very simply, "I want to take my half of the assets in our plantation and divide it, giving Kevin ownership of a quarter, and I will keep my quarter. No hard feelings." Michael asked Kevin if that was agreeable. He replied, "Yes." All the details were taken care of by Michael. As soon as Kevin moved out of Damian's room, he immediately began moving into Antwon's. Little did Damian know that Kevin had been having an affair with Antwon for several months and had kept it very low-key. Due to this, our living environment became extremely uncomfortable.

When Antwon was officially brought into the family, he was given one half of Dan's interest in the estate. So, he owned one-sixth of the estate. Dan's other quarter of the percent of the estate is held in limbo and holds an empty seat on the Board of Directors. His stock is in a blind trust and is voted by the president of the board. It is his decision and his decision alone. So, in reality, the president of the board is the only voting member that holds controlling interests in the plantation. And the current president is Damian.

Damian maintained the presidency of the plantation until the end of 1872. At that time, Michael and I had been together for ten years. The plantation had prospered under Damian's supervision. Antwon and Kevin were in charge of all crop operations, and each year they exceeded expectations. I managed the cattle operation and had secured a large contract with the United States Army providing them thousands of pounds of beef.

By the end of 1872, we had provided the Army with over 900 head of cattle. Replenishing our heard was now my immediate priority. At the same time, Michael's practice had expanded into the outskirts of New Orleans closest to our plantation. He had taken on several patients that had used Michael's old hospital but preferred his clinic instead. Our plantation was financially very solvent, and once again, the Jackson plantation became well known. Damian adjusted to the life of a bachelor. He developed an often sexual relationship with Bobby and William just to keep him occupied, but it was nothing more than sex. No emotions, just sexual lust. He seemed quite satisfied with that approach.

William and Bobby were performing their duties as our valets without any issues. The two of them shared a bedroom at the plantation, and at times Damian would join them for some hot three-way action before he retired for the evening. All in all, the plantation was functioning beautifully, and there were no significant issues. The years have been good to all of us, and when we sat down to have our nightly dinners, the four of us would discuss a range of topics from the plantation operation to past and present relationships that affect our personal lives.

Our mansion was so large that one could disappear for a day without being found. While construction may have added additional rooms, it also constructed extra-long hallways, secret compartments, and multiple ways to get anywhere in the house. It was like a maze if you were not familiar with it. This was perfectly suitable for William and Bobby. The two of them were like ghosts and had perfected their duties to the point that they become invisible in their service to Michael and me.

When we would return home from work at the end of the day, our clothes were laid out for the next day, our beds were turned down, and William and Bobby were nowhere to be found. Michael and I loved to enjoy our drinks in the parlor room. Without even a word, our drinks would be refilled, ready to enjoy, as if by magic. We were never bothered before our evening meals with Damian, Antwon, and Kevin; everything was served just the way we wanted, and far too often, it seemed like the meal of the day was what we had privately discussed. William and Bobby would instantly appear for just the table service, and soon after we finished our meal, they would vanish to the outer sanctum of the main house.

Many nights Damian would join either William or Bobby, sometimes both for a quick fling before retiring for the night. They usually found him in his room, which was conveniently connected to theirs. These flings became a common occurrence for Damian. He expressed a keen sexual interest in William because he seemed more stable and loving, plus younger and more energetic than Bobby. Bobby was more interested in just having a quick sexual encounter and getting on with it, while William, on the other hand, was into making deep and passionate love, which Damian found more appealing.

A lot can be said about the relationship that had grown between Kevin and Antwon, who paid little attention to William and Bobby. As long as I had known Kevin, I never once seen him truly invested in any one thing, so I admired how devoted he was to Antwon. His redneck ways from Kentucky always showed when we were riding the range, herding cows, talking over the campfire, or drinking with the plantation workers. He was like Dr. Jekyll and Mr. Hyde, when we were in the big house having dinner or drinks together, he was soft as an angel, delicate like a butterfly and as loving as a pussy cat. Many times we saw him with his arms around Antwon and the biggest smile anyone had ever seen on his face. Antwon was three inches taller than Kevin, and he could pick him up like a marshmallow if he so desired. I wondered in the privacy of their room which one was the top and who was the bottom, or did they alternate? I guessed in time that I might find out.

Bobby always took his overnight leave from the plantation and went into town. Nevertheless, he always reported back in time for his duties and shared his escapades from the night before. William would often caution Bobby to his numerous encounters while off the plantation and encouraged him to use discretion. Bobby's regular outings were brought to our attention, so we discussed with Damian to start using protection because he was having casual sex with both of them. Because Michael's medical practice had expanded into the outer reaches of New Orleans, he was aware of the spreading of the disease syphilis that has reached our surrounding area. This news startled Damian, and it became a topic of conversation at several of our nightly dinners.

I gave Bobby strict orders not to leave the plantation any more than once a week to go into New Orleans for his overnight encounters. He seemed to be lackadaisical about the information at hand. I talked to Michael about his reaction to my conversation with him and asked him if he would have a discussion with him about the medical complications of syphilis. Michael sat Bobby down one afternoon and described the symptoms of the disease, how it was transmitted and that he should use extreme caution during sex, for that syphilis was nearly incurable during this time. He also said that if he brought it back to the plantation and infected any member of our family, his position would be immediately and permanently terminated without question.

After Michael's discussion with Bobby, he curtailed his trips to New Orleans for some time. It seemed like everything was returning back to normalcy, and the two valets continued having their casual encounters with Damian whenever passions flared. William was still extremely cautious when having sex with Bobby; nothing changed with him. He routinely inspected his penis and manhole for any indication of disease, as Michael had instructed him before any encounter. William was insistent on maintaining a wholesome sexual environment in which to fully enjoy Damian without fear or any caution, just love.

With the help of Kevin, I have been fulfilling our annual beef cattle contract with the Army for three years now. To help build up our stock and selection, we employed the help of a breeder of young beef cattle about a hundred miles west of the plantation. He kept in stock a large variety of beef cattle from which we selected Angus, Hereford, and just a few longhorns just for show. Each spring, our field hands plus a few hired cowhands would drive a herd of approximately 350 to our plantation to help bolster our cattle production. Since it takes an average of 283 days for a heifer to give birth when gestated, we segregate our cattle into groups. These included our selective breeding show cattle, our rearing group where all the impregnated heifers laid, and then the free-range where the rest of the bovine grazed.

Our plantation employed about eighty field hands to work all areas of the plantation. It would take an entire season for us to fatten the cattle enough to be ready for sale to the Army. We were blessed to have a great advantage in that our pastures were more than adequately irrigated; we had plenty of grass to fatten our young heard in the shortest amount of time. We were generating an enormous profit on our cattle operation, and Kevin and I were immensely proud of this contribution to our plantation.

In keeping with our past tradition, we would sometimes go into New Orleans and have a drink at our favorite bar, The Rusty Nail, just for old times' sake. One night, while we were out having a drink there, a random stranger came up to us and introduced himself. He said, "Oh, so you're Jim, the former Sheriff of New Orleans."

I said, "Yes, what is your name, fella? He replied, "Forgive me, sir, where are my manners. My name is Steven Tyler Louis, the III. Now, you may not remember this, but you were the one who arrested me several years ago when you were just serving as the deputy of Treme and the surrounding counties. I was ill-fatedly involved in a bar fight that happened to fall on the outskirts of your patrol area. If you remember correctly, we had a long conversation, and we both walked down a back alley where I got on my knees and began to unzip your pants and attempted to give you pleasure. Unfortunately, you pushed me down in the pissy dirt, kicked me in the ribs, and said, 'Get on your way, you bastard… not today.'"

I said, "Well, Steve, I guess that was your lucky day. Now, what is it you need from us today, sir?"

"I hear you purchased a large plantation on the outskirts of New Orleans and are no longer in law enforcement." I held my glass and gently swirled my liquor and then said, "That is correct, and I guess it's time for you to be on your way, Steve, I don't think we have anything else to discuss."

Kevin just laughed and said nothing that exciting ever happened when he was on patrol. Steve smirked then quickly drew his pistol, aiming at my face. I just as quickly slammed my drink on the bar and knocked his arm, making him discharge his weapon just missing the bartender and me.

Within that split second, Kevin bounced up over my shoulder, aiming his pistol at his face, I snatched his gun and Kevin fired. Bang! The man screamed and held his ear that Kevin blew clean off. I finished my drink, slammed his pistol on the bar, and slowly stood up. "Now, are we finished, Mr. Louis?" He fearfully nodded and ran, his ear dripping blood all the way out the door.

Kevin and I finished a few more drinks before getting on our horses and riding back to the plantation to have dinner with the family. During dinner, I brought up the encounter with Steve at the Rusty Nail, and we all had a good laugh.

"You should have seen the guy's face before I nailed his ear to the wall! Ha-ha, He was grittn' his teeth like he could bite the sights of a six-gun," said Kevin. During our discussion, Bobby overheard Steve's name. He did not say anything then, but later that night, he asked me about the Rusty Nail and where it was located. I did not think much about it and gave him directions.

That particular bar had an interesting mix of clientele. Often times, both cowhands and farmhands from local plantations or ranches would come to town, looking for any type of sexual encounter that they can find. It is a perfect bar for a quick pick up if you know what I mean. But it also served the best whiskey in town, so against my better judgment, I was fond of this bar.

Damian had expanded the household staff to ten servants. Michael's mother now only supervised the kitchen staff as she was aging, and it was too difficult for her to perform many of the required functions of the chief cook. The kitchen staff consisted of three chefs: two entrée and one pastry. The remainder of the staff were housekeepers who took care of the large main house that was full of antiquities, silver and family heirlooms. William and Bobby only took care of Damian's bedroom and the bedroom that Michael and I share, for they were off-limits to the remainder of the rest of the staff.

Everyone knew that Damian had decisively organized the big house staffing operation. He planned out in great detail what tasks should be operated, when for how long, and knew when anything was not done correctly and by whom. In addition to organizing the big house, Damian took it upon himself to oversee the housing project for the plantation workers to ensure that their living standards were at a premium.

Michael's medical practice had grown so large that his medical suite at the plantation had reached capacity. At dinner one night, we discussed the possibility of expanding it with the addition of a research laboratory for there were so many new cases of disease being detected in New Orleans for which Michael did not always have a remedy. Frequently at night, my quality time together with Michael was now being interrupted with him studying medical and chemistry manuals trying to understand the newest treatments for these diseases that are appearing around town. He said that with a laboratory, he could experiment with various drugs and successfully treat more patients. So, we decided to expand his facility to include the laboratory and another surgical unit.

Antwon has turned out to be a real cowboy. Now about thirty-two years old, he could throw a lariat, ride a horse with his eyes closed, herd cattle, and keep up with Kevin every step of the way. His six-foot-three frame and slender build could handle every plantation duty that needed to be done. He detested Bobby nearly vehemently but had nothing but the utmost respect for William. He knew that Damian liked William and was overly concerned about Bobby's lackadaisical ways of life and his frequent overnight trips to New Orleans for whatever reason. He saw these self-indulged outings as a hindrance to Damian and William's relationship.

The construction for the expansion of Michael's medical suite was nearly completed in a little bit longer than six weeks. We hired a team of carpenters from the best firm in New Orleans to carry out the build. Michael had ordered all of the laboratory equipment from New York City, and it arrived a few days after the completion of the laboratory. It took about a week to fully set up his lab and restructure his medical office, but the finished product was a sight to behold! Now he can spend the majority of his free time testing various formulas and antidotes to treat any new diseases that he encountered in his practice. One of the most prevalent diseases that he wished to treat was syphilis, for, at this time, it had become rampant in the streets of New Orleans. All of the medical journals to date listed only two possible treatments to combat this disease. One, which was Mercury and the second, which was a formula called 606, would later be called Salvarsan.

Michael kept detailed records of all the patients that he treated for syphilis, mapping all the signs of outbreaks. He backtracked his patients' outings to various bars in the New Orleans area. Over time the largest percentage of the new cases could be pinpointed to the Rusty Nail bar where cowboys and ranch hands frequented for anonymous sex. Michael also remembered that Kevin and I brought up that bar before at one of our dinners a few months ago. He discussed his findings with me, and I told him that Bobby had inquired as to its location, and at that time, I didn't think anything about it. I told him we need to talk with the entire household, especially Bobby. Michael agreed and said that we should do it immediately after work tomorrow, for he had a light day.

Sunday afternoon fell upon us, Michael was in his clinic, and Bobby suddenly dipped his head in and asked Michael if he could talk to him about a medical issue. Michael said, "Certainly, Bobby, that is what I'm here for." Bobby went on to say that he was having quite some irritation around his rectum, and he would like Michael to check it out. As soon as Michael saw Bobby's rectum and noticed the chancres surrounding it, he knew that Bobby had syphilis. As Bobby was lying naked from the waist down on Michael's treatment table, Michael told him just to lay there for a minute, for he'd be right back.

Michael came into the main house and grabbed me by my arm and said, "Follow me." He told me of his discovery and that Bobby's disease is so contagious that it could easily be spread to Damian and William and if he has not already, to others on the plantation. I told Michael that I had already warned Bobby that if he ever bought this disease into our family, his position would be terminated on the spot. Michael agreed wholeheartedly. But first, he said, we have to get this treated and all of us, excluding you and I, need to be inspected to ensure that has not turned into an epidemic on our plantation. Bobby was treated with Michael's latest formula for syphilis, hoping that it either cured the infection or possibly curtail the spread of it within his body. He told Bobby that he needs to come back for follow-up treatments at least once a week for three weeks to see if any improvement has been made.

After Bobby was treated, Michael summoned Damian to the clinic. He informed Damian of his findings and that syphilis was an almost untreatable and genuinely frightening disease, and that it was currently rampant here in New Orleans. Damian was irate. He came to me immediately and wanted to know what we were going to do with Bobby.

I told him, "I had already informed Bobby that his position would be terminated long ago if he ever bought this disease into the family. So, please have Michael check you out as well as William to see what the prognosis is, then we will make our decision accordingly to Michael's medical advice."

Michael completed his medical examination for both men. Luckily for Damian and William, Michael did not detect any chancres on either of them. He inquired as to the type of sex they primarily had with Bobby, and both of them indicated that they did not pursue his manhole for pleasure. Michael said, well, that's good news, for you have to come in direct contact with an open wound or sexual fluids for risk of infection. And if you and William were the only ones to have made sexual demands in that area, you should be okay, but from now on, both of you should use condoms, which will ensure safe sex. And just in case either of you was exposed, you two should have frequent checkups with me for at least a month to be on the safe side.

Damian inquired as to what condoms were, and Michael explained that he could make them out of goatskin and showed Damian drawings of them. He showed him that they were placed over the penis for protection and worn while inserting your member into your partner's cavity. Damian was more than agreeable. Michael then explained how to use the condom to William, who was just as agreeable as Damian had been to its usage.

During the next three weeks, while Bobby was being treated, Michael made a trip to New Orleans and spoke to the Chief Medical Officer for the city. He informed him of his findings and that the Rusty Nail was the epicenter for the majority of the syphilis cases that he had treated in his clinic. Michael recommended to the Chief Medical Officer that he should push the city council to close the bar to stop the spread of this disease in New Orleans. He agreed to shut down the Rusty Nail immediately. He posted a quarantine sign stating the reason why it was closed, also saying that anyone who frequents the establishment should seek medical counsel as soon as possible. After three weeks had passed, Bobby was terminated, and no further cases of syphilis were detected on the plantation. Bobby, however, was the direct cause of eleven cases on the neighboring plantations, and if we had not fired him, we would have feared for his safety.

Damian and William now visibly appeared more affectionate toward one another. With Bobby out of the picture, we replaced him with another valet, and William took residence in Damian's room. William's duties, for the time being, were not changed, but before and after work, he was treated as a friend of the family. William and Damian's relationship grew stronger by the day. One night over dinner, Damian suggested that we promote William to the head butler for the plantation. We all agreed that he had matured into a knowledgeable and trustworthy individual who is an essential part of the proper functioning of the big house. Damian assured us that he would take full responsibility for William and that he was extremely happy with him as his partner in life. Michael and I had not seen this much happiness in Damian's eyes since he and Dan were last together; it warmed our hearts.

Over fifteen years have come and gone since my journey began in the military to my life now on the plantation. Michael and I have been together for fourteen years now. We have seen happiness, sadness and grief. Together we have seen the rise and fall of the Jackson plantation and its rebirth again. Today, the Jackson plantation has exceeded all its former glory and is out-producing the old plantation in North Carolina tenfold. The original cannot even compare to the new main house. Damian has ensured that its beauty is a shining tribute to the power couple of New Orleans. And If you have noticed, we always make all of our major decisions over dinner. One night while we were all together, we discussed how much Antwon has contributed to the success of the plantation. Damian still owns the controlling interest of Dan's quarter of the estate, and we all agreed that Antwon should receive it. Now Kevin and Antwon together will own 25% of the Jackson plantation, and with their profits, they can forge a new life together.

Happiness in life is never a guarantee for this was evident with our past relationships, but love has always been our ultimate goal. Each of us may have taken a different path; Michael and I were fortunate enough to find exactly what we always needed from the very beginning. From the battle of Antietam to the operating table where we were sewn together for life. What a loving journey this has been, never a curse word or heated disagreement. And even now, with our more secluded lifestyle, we still remained the power couple of New Orleans. Damian sadly enough lost his brother Dan, which he loved dearly. However, in the final days, he found William, who matured into a man equal to his status on the plantation. Damian also decided to give him his last name of Jefferson, as well as one-quarter of his holdings, so together they own 25%.

As you picture the new Jackson plantation with all its lush grassy acres, massive plantation house sitting on the outskirts of New Orleans, one of the ten best plantations in Louisiana, a person must have a thorough understanding of the gay hands that it took to build it. In the years ahead, newspaper articles from all over the state will be dedicated to the history of the "power couple's" family unit that established one of the most extravagant and stateliest plantations in the state of Louisiana. To this date, there was never an eyebrow raised in the state of Louisiana as to who Kevin, Antwon, Damian, William, Michael or I were. We are southern royalty. We are the Jacksons.

The End

References

o Ogden, Maurice. *The Hangman*. Published for Regina Publications by Media Masters, 1968.

JAMES MARQUIS

*J*ames was born the son of sharecroppers and grew up in tenement housing on a farm in Iroquois County, Illinois. At the age of thirteen, he and his family moved to a small village in the same county where he graduated high school. At the age of seventeen, he moved from the small village to Champaign, Illinois, the home of the University of Illinois, and he secured a position as a teller at one of the major banks. Because of his "Personality, Looks and Communication Skills," it was not long before he was promoted to head teller. It was during this time frame that he was drafted into the Army to supplement the surge of troops during the Vietnamese crisis.

His distinguished military career was recognized when he received a Bronze Star Medal. His training in the Army prepared him to pursue his life's dream of acquiring financial freedom. After he was discharged from the Army, he returned to the small Illinois bank and discovered it had limited promotional opportunities for him to achieve his dream.

James sought out and attained a position with one of the world's largest banks based in California, where he spent twenty-five years. During this time, he was recognized internationally as the bank's top motivational speaker. In the last ten years of his employment, he attained a level of Regional Vice President of Operations for northern California.

He was influenced to put his writing talents in book form by the author, Annie Prouix, who wrote the book "Brokeback Mountain." James is also writing a fictional love story entitled "1968: A Vietnam War Love Story," which was influence by some events that took place before, during, and after his tour of duty in Vietnam.